CRAVED—TRIBUTE BRIDES OF THE DREXIAN WARRIORS #8

A SCI-FI ALIEN WARRIOR ROMANCE

TANA STONE

BROADMOOR BOOKS

She thinks the gorgeous, silver fox alien is a hologram. He's not.

The only alien warrior True isn't intimidated by is the one in her holodeck simulation. Not only is True a virgin, she's barely been kissed, so the huge, hunky Drexian warriors terrify her. But the guy in her simulation doesn't. He may be as big and built as the rest of them, but she knows he's not real. It's the only reason she's not afraid to kiss him.

Captain Varden never meant to lie to True, but when she assumed he was a hologram, he didn't correct her. Especially not after she laid that kiss on him. Now she's convinced he isn't real, which is probably for the best. He's too old for someone as young and pretty as her, although when she kisses him he feels like a Drexian cadet again.

When the Kronock attack and they're forced to abandon the space station, True comes face-to-face with her hologram—on the escape transport. Before she can be properly outraged, they're stranded on a jungle planet. Between trying to stay alive and evading the enemy, can she forgive him for deceiving her? Can he ever accept that she could fall for someone so much older?

This standalone alien abduction romance novel features steamy scenes on a jungle planet, action-packed space battles, smoking-hot Drexian warriors who will do anything to protect the women they love, and a guaranteed HEA. If you like silver foxes, aliens with extra erogenous zones, and virgins getting (a lot) more than they bargained for, you'll love CRAVED, the eighth book in Tana Stone's sci-fi romance Tribute Brides of the Drexian Warriors series.

CHAPTER
ONE

Captain Varden ran a hand across the scruff that he'd let grow on his face over the past several days. Usually, he was clean-shaven, but he hadn't left the bridge of the space station since he'd gotten word of the possible attack by the Drexians' dreaded enemy, the Kronock. Although he'd never worn a beard, he knew his facial hair would have the same traces of silver that shot through the hair at his temples. Not that he could worry about that now, or the fact that he must have looked as exhausted as he felt.

He swallowed hard and peered up at the screens suspended overhead, tapping the toe of his boot against the metal floor and hearing the hollow echo over the usual sounds of computers beeping, fingers tapping on screens, and static transmissions. He'd been captain of the Drexians' high-tech space station—also known as the Boat—for almost two decades, but he'd never had to deal with something quite like this before. Since the Boat was used primarily as a place to bring Earth females to be matched with Drexian warriors—and it came complete with holographic fantasy suites, alien wedding planners, and even holodecks for honeymoons—military defense had never been a major issue. Until now.

1

His people's mortal enemy, the Kronock, had recently been testing the station's defenses. Between sabotage and outright attacks, they'd shown that they were no longer technologically inferior monsters. They had adapted and they had evolved, and none of it boded well for the Drexians who'd pledged to keep Earth safe from their violence. He rocked back on his heels as he scanned the readouts. Where were they?

After doubling the space station's patrols and adding even more officers to monitor long-range sensors, there had been nothing. The invasion should have happened by now, but after initial intelligence reports the day of the Boat's holiday party, there had been virtual silence. Instead of feeling relieved, Varden felt a gnawing sense of impending doom.

"Incoming transmission from former high commander Kax." One of his officers turned from where he stood at a glossy ebony console.

Varden nodded. "On screen."

The Drexian warrior's face appeared above him—vivid green eyes narrowed in obvious concern. "Captain, we've been able to track down the Kronock fleet."

Varden clasped his hands behind his back. Kax had taken a small group of intelligence officers to track and gather information on the Kronock movements. He knew the warrior was skilled in slipping in and out of Kronock territory undetected—using stealth as opposed to brute force.

"Brother!"

The captain didn't need to turn to know that the Drexian who'd entered the bridge was Kax's younger brother, Dorn. With his deep, booming voice and pounding footfall, the former commander of Inferno Force was the definition of brute force. He looked it, too— dark hair hanging loose around his neck, tattoos peeking from underneath the arms of a tight black T-shirt, and a face full of stubble.

He gave Varden a chest salute when he reached him, then

pivoted back to face his brother on the screen. "What have you discovered?"

The corners of Kax's mouth twitched, but he restrained himself from whatever comment he wished to make about his younger, impetuous brother. The captain had been witness to enough arguments between the two to know that the only thing they seemed to share was the color of their eyes—and their loyalty to the Drexian empire.

"Not good news, I'm afraid," Kax said, his face losing any trace of amusement. "We got reports of them massing ships within an asteroid belt near Talaurus II."

Dorn grunted. "*Grek*. Since when are these scaly monsters strategic?"

"I think we've learned that our enemies are not what we'd been led to believe," Kax said.

"What *they'd* led us to believe," Varden added.

After nearly thirty human years of skirmishes with a technologically outmatched rival, the Drexians had discovered that the Kronock had been secretly developing weapons and high-powered ships—some with the aid of Drexian traitors. Now, the enemy was a formidable opponent.

"Does it look like they're preparing for battle?" Dorn asked.

Kax gave a curt shake of his head. "It looks like they're prepping for war."

Varden's stomach tightened into an even harder knot. "What about the earlier reports that the Boat is their target?"

"Their end game is Earth, but from the chatter we've picked up, they want to strike a blow to the Drexian empire we won't soon forget." Kax pressed his mouth into a hard line. "They want to take all our human mates."

Dorn growled. "Over my dead body."

"I believe that is the idea," his brother said, then shifted his eyes to the captain. "We couldn't get close enough to lay eyes on the fleet, but our sources say they have at least a dozen battleships."

Varden remembered what had happened when a Kronock battleship had jumped in and fired on the Boat. "We're no match for their firepower." He thought about the three Inferno Force battleships that had arrived to flank the station. "And we'd be outnumbered."

"No one can outfight Inferno Force," Dorn said.

The fiercest fighting force in the Drexian empire—and arguably the galaxy—Inferno Force had never lost a battle against the Kronock. Until just a few days ago.

"Inferno Force is still spread throughout the empire," Kax said. "Even if we could get them all to you in time, that would leave planets and colonies undefended."

"What is more important than Earth?" Dorn asked, his voice growing louder.

"On that, you and I agree," Kax said. "Earth must be defended at all costs."

Since the Drexians had stopped producing enough of their own females to continue their species, they'd relied on their compatibility with humans and the deal they'd made with Earth decades earlier. If the planet was destroyed or invaded and harvested, as the Kronock liked to do, that would mean the end of the Drexians taking tribute brides from Earth as mates for their warriors. Eventually, it would mean the end of the Drexians altogether.

"Then the answer is clear," Varden said, the realization hitting him as if he'd been doused with freezing water. "We must abandon the Boat and get the women to safety."

Dorn swung his head to face Varden. "Leave the Boat?"

Kax closed his eyes briefly, then nodded. "The captain is right. It's the only way to ensure the humans aren't taken by the Kronock. Then Inferno Force can focus its attention on repelling and destroying instead of defending."

Dorn opened his mouth to argue, then his shoulders sagged. "You are both right. Keeping the females safe and protecting Earth is more important than the station."

"I'll begin evacuation protocol," Varden said.

Dorn clapped a hand on his shoulder without a word and strode off the bridge.

"I am sorry," Kax said.

Varden nodded. "I will send you the rendezvous coordinates on an encrypted channel so you and your team can meet us there." Before Kax could ask, Varden added, "I will make sure your mate is on a transport with one of our medics."

Kax gave him a grateful smile. "I know she's early in the pregnancy, but..."

"No need to explain," Varden said, watching the warrior's jaw relax before he signed off and the screen went blank.

The bridge was nearly silent for a moment as all the officers turned toward him. They'd heard the transmission and knew what it meant. He raised his eyes and nodded to his first officer, Kos. "Begin evacuation proceedings."

The warrior's eyes were wide, but he straightened his shoulders. "Yes, sir."

Varden fought back a wave of nausea at the thought of the station he'd captained for so long being destroyed. Glancing around the gleaming metal and black of the bridge where he'd spent so many hours, he let out a breath to steady himself. It was the right call, although he hated to make it.

As a Drexian warrior, he'd been trained to handle battles. Before rising to the rank of captain and taking command of the Boat, he'd fought in countless battles against the Kronock. He did not fear a fight. What he feared was putting the residents of the space station at risk, specifically the human women who'd been taken from Earth to be brides for his species. Even more specifically, he feared for the safety of one human. True.

He knew he had no claim to her, but he could not help thinking of the pretty, golden-haired human. Not only was he not on the list to receive a tribute bride, True wasn't even a tribute bride. Not anymore. She lived in the independent section of the station with the other humans who'd rejected the concept of taking an alien warrior mate. He knew all that logically, but it didn't matter to his heart.

Since the day he'd stumbled into her holodeck program—to be fair, the day he'd used his override commands to sneak in—and she'd assumed he was a holographic character, Varden had been obsessed with her. It didn't help that she'd kissed him—the best kiss of his life—before running off down the holographic beach.

He'd thought of little else since that day, and he'd conspired to join her on the holodeck every time she was there, although he'd yet to build up the courage to tell her that he wasn't a figment of light and energy beams. He didn't want to ruin her escape, since he knew she used the peaceful ocean setting to get away from the realities of being abducted from Earth and taken to live on a high-tech alien space station. At least that's what he told himself every time he failed to confess the truth. The reality was that he was enjoying the fantasy too much to risk spoiling it. The time he spent with her walking on the beach was the happiest he'd ever been, and he knew that would all change the second she realized he was a flesh-and-blood Drexian.

Just thinking about her standing on the edge of the water, the breeze blowing her hair back as she laughed, made his cock twitch. He'd never considered taking a tribute bride for himself—he had long since passed the window for that—but his desire for this timid human who usually avoided contact with anyone but other independent females was overpowering.

Now, even though his thoughts should be solely on the evacuation of the Boat, he couldn't help thinking about her and worrying about her safety. He'd put one of his best officers in charge of shepherding the females in the independent section to safety.

Taking long steps toward his first officer, he rested a hand on the warrior's shoulder. "Contact Dakar and Vox. Assign them the task of getting the females from the independent side of the station into a transport ship along with the tribute brides."

"I'm assuming you wish those women to depart after the tributes."

Varden shook his head. "No. Send them together. All humans have equal priority on this station."

Kos cocked an eyebrow but began quickly swiping his fingers across his console to send the messages. The captain knew it was out of the ordinary to consider the women who'd rejected their Drexian mates to be in the same category as the tribute brides who had agreed to the deal, but he didn't care. He wasn't taking any chances with True's safety. He also knew that Dakar and Vox would take their job seriously, since their own mates had been independents before falling for their respective Drexians.

The independents who'd changed their minds and taken Drexian mates lit the smallest flicker of hope within Varden. If Ella and Shreya—both staunch independents—had changed their minds, then maybe True would, as well.

She still wouldn't choose a hologram, he reminded himself. *And that's what she thinks you are. A creation of light pulses.*

He couldn't help wondering what would happen when they all got off the station and were gathered at the Drexian colony rendezvous point. He'd managed to hide his identity from her on the Boat because it was such a massive station, and they moved in very different areas. But a colony was different. And there would be no holodeck.

He remembered the last time he'd been with True in her "Gulf of Mexico" simulation. They'd been sitting side by side in the sand, her in a flower-print dress and him in his Kranji uniform, since that was what he'd been wearing the first time he'd entered the program, and she thought that was what he'd been programmed to wear. The waves had been rolling in and barely lapping at their bare toes.

"I don't know what I'd do if I didn't have this...and you," she said, not taking her blue eyes off the water. "Sometimes the idea of being alone on an alien space station forever is a lot to handle."

"You aren't alone."

"I know." She twirled a strand of hair around one finger. "The station is packed with people and aliens, but eventually everyone pairs off. My best friend, Ella, lives with Dakar in the officers' section, and even Shreya moved over there with Vox. Who knows? Maybe this is a trend, and every independent will end up hooking up with a Drexian except me."

"Why not you?" He'd been curious about whether the idea of an alien repulsed her. "You do not find Drexians appealing?"

True giggled. "This would be a really weird conversation if you were actually real." She glanced at him. "Obviously, I find them attractive. I mean, you're incredibly hot. It's just..." Her cheeks flushed. "I can't."

"Why not?" He took her hand and stroked his thumb gently over the back of it.

Before she'd told him, the holodeck had beeped to let her know the time was up, and she'd dashed off. But not before giving him a kiss that he'd felt all the way to his toes. Now he may never know why True felt that she couldn't take a mate.

His first officer cleared his throat, and Varden looked down to where he was massaging the man's shoulder. Jerking his hand away, he mumbled an apology and stepped back.

Maybe it was just as well he wouldn't be able to continue whatever was going on with True. His craving for the woman was driving him mad.

CHAPTER
TWO

True flipped her hair off her shoulder as she glanced back. Good. No one saw her leave the independent section.

The last thing she needed was one of her friends asking her where she was going again. She knew she'd been spending a lot of time on the holodeck lately, but she had a good explanation. At least, it sounded good when she explained it to herself.

"It's stress relief," she whispered. That's what she'd tell anyone who asked. That's what she'd told her best friend, Ella, when she'd hit her up for her holodeck access code again.

She hurried down the wide corridor toward the inclinator. It was still early enough that the space station was yet to be bustling with activity, and she hoped the holodecks would be empty. Even with a special access code, she knew she wasn't supposed to take time from a tribute bride or a Drexian warrior, but she really needed to get into her simulation. The stress-relief line wasn't a total lie.

"After everything that's happened on the station and then what happened with Shreya," she said to Ella, "the ocean calms me down."

Ella hadn't pressed her too much, knowing that her friend took

9

things to heart and did tend to let external stress eat away at her. What True hadn't said was that the part of the holographic simulation that relieved her stress most wasn't the view of the Gulf of Mexico; it was the hunky holographic guy Ella had programmed into it for her.

At first she'd been startled that Ella had presumed to stick a guy in her perfect beach setting, especially since she knew that most men scared True. And she hadn't designed a mild-mannered dork that would have been completely non-threatening. Nope, typical Ella had given her a tall, muscular Drexian warrior with dark hair flecked with pewter at the temples. She'd decked him out in a martial arts uniform, since she knew True's guilty pleasure was old Jean-Claude Van Damme movies, and had even made him left-handed, a turn-on True herself couldn't explain.

Knowing Ella, this was her way of helping her friend get over her fear of Drexian men. True had to admit, it wasn't a bad plan. Since she knew he wasn't real, she'd felt comfortable talking to him and even kissing him.

Oh, yeah. The kissing was the best part. Her fingers tingled as she stepped onto the empty inclinator and thought back to his soft lips against hers. Leaning back against the compartment wall as it surged up, True closed her eyes and sank fully into the memory.

For a light projection, he felt incredibly real. Then again, the holographic technology on the alien space station was impressive, and she knew a lot of what she'd seen since she'd been on board was merely a clever manipulation of energy and light. She guessed she was lucky to be best friends with Ella, who was one of the ones who designed the holographic projections, and lucky the woman turned her talents from holographic wedding decor to creating the perfect man for True.

The doors of the inclinator slid open, and she walked quickly, her strappy pink sandals tapping on the shiny white floors. She'd almost reached the recreational holodeck wing when she heard fast footsteps behind her and a high-pitched voice.

"True?"

She paused and forced a smile onto her face as she turned around. "Hey, Cerise. What are you doing up so early?"

The Perogling only reached her waist, and half of that height seemed to be her tall wig of towering pink curls. A wide grin spread across the tiny alien's face, her bright coral lipstick a contrast to her iridescent pale blue skin.

"I'm meeting Serge and Reina. We're starting with our first of the new tribute brides today."

She tried not to stare at the creature's orange and hot-pink suit with wide piping at the lapels. Someone was definitely trying to emulate Serge's fashion sense, or lack thereof.

"That's right." True remembered hearing something about the recent transport of humans. Because of all the turmoil, it had been several weeks since any women had arrived on the station, and she knew a lot of the aliens on board were glad to have things returning to normal.

She had decidedly mixed feelings about the whole tribute bride thing. On the one hand, she appreciated the Drexians defending Earth from alien invaders. On the other, she still hadn't completely gotten over the shock of being abducted and brought to a high-tech space station hidden behind one of Saturn's moons. Luckily, she'd had the option of rejecting her Drexian match and going to live with the other humans who'd rejected the concept.

"What are you doing?" Cerise asked, eyeing the pink-and-yellow-striped dress that barely reached her knees. "Is there a party I don't know about?"

True tried to laugh, but it sounded choked. "No, I'm just getting a little change of scenery." She dragged her sweaty palms down her skirt and tried to change the subject. "Do you know much about the new women?"

Luckily, Cerise was easily distracted and obviously excited about the tribute brides. She nodded, and her wig bobbed. "The first one is from a place on Earth called New Zeen-land. Her name is Hope."

"New Zealand," True said, grinning as she corrected the alien. "I've heard it's beautiful there."

Cerise angled her head. "Is it far from your home?"

"Far from Alabama?" She laughed. "Yeah, you could say that."

"So you have never been to New Zeen…"

The two women stepped to one side as a group of Drexian warriors rushed by, all swiping at tablets and discussing something in low, urgent tones.

"New Zealand. Nope, I never traveled outside the Deep South until I came here."

"Is the Deep South a country?"

"More like a state of being," True said, this time without laughing. "There are some great things about it and some not-so-great things."

Cerise nodded solemnly. "Do you miss it?"

True thought for a moment. She'd definitely taken a while to adjust to life on the Boat, and there were things from Earth she missed, like real Coke from a bottle and buttermilk biscuits, but would she go back home if she could?

"No. As crazy as it is to be living on an alien space station, I like the life I've created here." She winked at Cerise. "And the friends I've made."

Since Shreya had rescued Cerise from an alien bordello, she'd been living with the independent humans and had fit in perfectly, despite the fact that she was far from human and was the only one of her species on board.

The Perogling's pale blue cheeks flushed pink. "I couldn't imagine living in the independent section without you."

The Drexian True recognized as Commander Dorn passed them without looking up, his strides long and his expression stormy. It looked like someone wasn't having a great morning.

Cerise jumped and retrieved a communication device from her

pocket. "Oh no." Her lips puckered as she read the screen. "It looks like I'm late, and the human from New Zeen, New Zleen...the human named Hope isn't adjusting so well."

True cringed, thinking back to her own hysterical screaming and crying when she'd finally been convinced she was living among aliens. "Good luck."

Cerise gave her an absent wave over her shoulder as she rushed off in the opposite direction.

Better her than me, True thought, and wondered if the independent section might get a new resident from New Zealand soon. It would be nice to have a new friend. She continued walking to the holodeck wing, grateful to find it empty.

She took a deep breath and smoothed down the front of her sundress. She always dressed for the beach, even if she sometimes felt silly walking around the station in sandals and summery dresses. *He* liked the dresses. At least that's what he'd said the last time she was here, and he'd run a finger underneath one of the spaghetti straps and let it drop down her shoulder.

Even thinking about it made her heart beat faster. It was the closest she'd ever come to being undressed by a man. She gave her head a shake and punched in the access code Ella had given her.

Don't be silly. He's not real.

Not that it mattered to her. He was the closest thing to a boyfriend she'd ever had. Growing up in a strict, religious household, she and her sisters had been prohibited from dating, dancing, drinking, and even showing a hint of skin. The idea of a gorgeous, massive man—check that, alien— kissing her would have made her mother pass out cold and her father run for his shotgun.

She couldn't help smiling wickedly at the thought of her parents if they could see her now—with her hair flowing loose and wearing a dress that showed off her legs and arms. It would serve them right for believing that awful neighbor girl over her.

When snot-nosed Missy Barnett had claimed to have seen True kissing a boy at school, her parents hadn't believed her. They'd actually believed Missy, since her father was a deacon in their church, and they'd kicked True out of their house. She'd been barely eighteen when she'd found herself homeless and hitchhiking to Mobile, Alabama in search of a job.

"Wonder what would have happened if the abnormally large guy hadn't stopped for me?" she murmured to herself as she waited for her holograph simulation to load. She knew now that the oddly large man had been a Drexian on a mission to procure human females without strong social ties. Since she'd been homeless and looking for a ride on the highway, that had been her.

Almost two years later, she'd still never kissed a man. A real man, at least, although she thought all the practice she was getting on the holodeck had to count for something. Not that she knew what she was practicing for. It wasn't like she would ever take a Drexian mate. They were just too huge.

She'd never gotten "the talk" growing up, but she'd gathered enough from Ella and the other women on the station to be petrified of sex with a Drexian. She knew the alien warriors were massive *everywhere*, and even experienced women had a period of adjustment. The thought of it made a virgin like her break out in a cold sweat.

No, she was just fine making out with her holographic guy, thank you very much.

The doors slid open, and she felt an immediate sense of calm as the scent of saltwater drifted out. Slipping off her shoes, she stepped inside and began walking toward the water, her feet sinking into the powdery sand. The ocean seemed especially blue today, the bright sun bouncing off the surface and making it glisten so brightly she had to shield her eyes. Seagulls swooped low and dipped their feet into the water before pulling up and arching high into the sky.

When she reached the edge of the water, she stopped and let the waves roll over her feet, the cool water bubbling up around her ankles. The sound of the water lapping against the sand drained all the stress from her body, and her shoulders relaxed as she tipped her face up to the sun, closing her eyes and breathing deeply.

After a moment, she opened her eyes and looked down the beach. Usually, by this point he'd joined her. Holding a hand over her eyes, she stared down in both directions, but all she could see was an unending stretch of white sand.

Where was he?

CHAPTER

THREE

Varden rocked back on his heels. The evacuation was going as well as could be expected.

He'd gotten some push-back from Serge, one of the station's wedding planners, who'd insisted that the evacuation was ruining his ability to convince the new tribute brides that life among aliens would be safe and idyllic. The little Gatazoid had actually shown up on the bridge stamping his platform shoes—his usually blue hair completely pink—and insisting that they stop upsetting his brides.

"I don't know who was in charge of procuring the female from New Zealand, but she has no intention of going along with anything easily," Serge said. "And if I have to tell her that instead of a holographic fantasy suite, she has to be crammed onto an escape transport, I might just lose her to the independent side."

Varden stared at Serge, trying not to laugh as the alien waved his hands over his head. "It can't be helped. Would you prefer the tribute brides get taken by the Kronock when they invade?"

Serge's eyes had grown even larger than usual. "They're invading? Now? No one told me that. They said preventative measures. An invasion is an entirely different matter."

Varden nodded. "Invasion."

Serge had gone pale and spun on his heel, shrieking for Cerise and Reina as he dashed off the bridge.

Varden shook his head, glad that the tribute brides, along with their wedding planners and handlers, were now safely on a transport. Approximately half the station's residents had already departed, and the others were being herded into the transports.

Walking over to the nearest officer, he looked over the Drexian's shoulder at the console readouts. "Any report from Dakar and Vox?"

The warrior scanned the screen. "Affirmative. They are moving the residents of the independent wing to the hangar bay now."

Varden let out a sigh of relief. "Can you confirm that all of the humans from that section are with them?"

"Yes, sir." The Drexian tapped on his screen while Varden walked back to his post, tilting his head back to watch the view screen and the massive Inferno Force battleships moving away from them and closer to Earth.

He still hated sacrificing the Boat, but he knew it was necessary. Perhaps the Kronock wouldn't destroy the station when they realized it had been abandoned. But knowing how the vicious aliens reveled in destruction, he doubted it.

"Report from Dakar, Captain," the officer said. "They cannot locate one of the humans."

Varden's gut clenched before he even asked the question. "Do they have a name for the missing female?"

"Dakar says it is his mate's friend, True."

Grek.

"His mate wants to leave the group and go look for her. Dakar is asking for permission to leave Vox in charge and go with his mate."

"Negative," Varden said. "I need him to get those women off the station. Can you tell me if any of the holodecks are currently occupied?"

The officer tapped the console. "Affirmative. One is currently running a program."

"Even after the evacuation announcements?"

"I'm afraid we've been having trouble with communications within the holodecks, sir. A side effect of the damage done to the station during the last attack, I'm sure."

Varden scowled. "So she doesn't know...I mean, whoever is inside the simulation has no idea we're abandoning ship?"

"That is correct, Captain. Do you think the missing human is in there?"

Varden didn't answer him. He knew she was, but he wasn't sending Dakar to retrieve her. "Tell Dakar I will personally locate her. He is to proceed with his evacuation of the humans."

His first officer swiveled to face him. "Sir?"

He ignored the curious glances coming from his bridge officers as he looked pointedly at Kos. "You have the bridge until I return. If you do not hear from me and all the residents have evacuated, I trust you to get the bridge crew onto a transport off the station."

"Without you?"

"I will come as soon as I locate the missing human."

"But sir." His first officer sounded as confused as he looked. "You're leaving overseeing the evacuation of the station because one human is—?"

"I said, I will be back." He leveled his gaze at Kos. "Do you not feel yourself capable of handling the bridge in my absence?"

The Drexian's face colored. "Of course not. I mean, of course I do, sir."

"Good." Varden nodded. "I know the station is in good hands."

With that, he turned and walked swiftly from the bridge, waiting until the doors had swished shut to break into a run. His boots thudded against the floor as he ran down the halls, empty except for Drexians making final checks of rooms. They saluted him as he passed, although they seemed startled to see him running.

He found an open inclinator compartment and jumped in, swiping his hand over a side panel and willing it to go faster as the doors slid closed and it dropped down. The soft pulsing light and instrumental music did nothing to calm him as he waited impatiently for the doors to open again.

This was his fault. He'd been so distracted by the news from Kax and the evacuation, he hadn't even checked the alerts he'd set to tell him every time the holodecks were being used. It was how he'd been able to join her each time she activated the "Gulf of Mexico" simulation.

Of course, if he'd been honest with her from the beginning, he wouldn't have had to set alerts and sneak around pretending to be a hologram. And now he was going to terrify her by revealing that not only was he not a hologram, he was the station's captain, and they needed to evacuate before they were invaded by the Kronock.

"This should go over well," he muttered to himself as the inclinator doors opened, and he burst out into the corridor.

He only passed a few straggling residents in the corridor—a pair of Vexlings, a lone Neebix, and a nervous-looking Gatazoid—all of whom he instructed to proceed immediately to the hangar bay. When he rounded the corner to the holodeck wing, he stopped short.

"Aren't you the Perogling who returned with Vox and Shreya?"

The alien in the tall wig nodded. "Cerise. Aren't you the captain?"

"Varden." He glanced up at the holodeck displays and noticed that one was running. "Why are you here?"

She wrung her hands and pointed to the nearest holodeck doors. "My friend went in there, but I can't find a way to go in and let her know about the evacuation."

Varden stepped up to the controls, assessing instantly that bridge communications had been damaged. His heart hammered in his chest as he imagined True being stuck inside, and he wondered how long it would take him to batter down the doors. Typing in his command override code, he disabled the locks, letting out a breath of relief when it worked.

Cerise clapped as the holodeck doors slid open. Before either of them could rush inside, the station shuddered and the lights overhead flickered.

The Kronock.

Varden cursed to himself as another impact almost knocked him off his feet. Cerise fell and began sliding as the station tilted to one side. Grabbing her by the ankle, he pulled her back and helped her stand.

"Stay right here," he said to the wide-eyed alien. "I'll get True."

He didn't wait for her response, running into the simulation and feeling his boots sink into the sand. Scanning the space, he saw True standing at the edge of the water with her head lifted toward the sun. For a moment, he wanted to preserve the moment in his mind—her so pretty and carefree as the water swirled around her feet and him still a holographic fantasy. The moment before she discovered the truth. But there wasn't time.

"True!" he called out as the station shook again.

She turned and saw him, her face breaking into a smile before her gaze dropped to his uniform. "What—?"

"I'm sorry," he said, running up and taking her by the hand. "There isn't time to explain. The station is under attack. We need to leave."

Happiness turned to confusion turned to mistrust. She tried to pull her hand away from him. "Who are you? What's going on?"

The scene around them flickered, the blue sky becoming white holographic tiles for a moment. "If we don't leave now, there's a chance we won't be able to get off the station before the Kronock either board it and take us captive or blow us all to bits."

Her pretty pink mouth opened and closed.

"Hurry!" Cerise screamed from the doorway, poking her head inside.

"Please, True," he begged.

She pressed her lips together, but she nodded, letting him pull her with him as he ran out of the holodeck. Cerise was already running ahead and waving for them to catch up, and he and True ran quickly as the corridor lights spluttered off and on.

"Too dangerous," he yelled when Cerise headed for an inclinator. Instead, he led them to a hidden stairwell that spiraled down into the station. "The hangar bay is only one level down."

He let the women descend in front of him, holding tight to the railing as the station rumbled from another impact. When they reached the level below, he reached for True's hand, but she pulled it away.

Cerise waved them both forward. "Hangar bay!"

They burst through the double doors, with Varden scanning the near-empty space for a transport.

"Captain!" His first officer was standing at the entrance ramp of a battered ship. "I've been holding it for you."

Varden wondered if this was the oldest ship in the Drexian fleet as he and the women ran on board and the ramp lifted behind them. Kos already had the ship lifting off as he fell into the copilot's chair next to him.

The ship rocketed out of the hangar bay and shot away from the station, banking hard and flying behind the station to avoid Kronock fire. When they'd gone to warp speed, Varden let out a breath. "Nice flying, Officer."

"Thank you, Captain."

Swiveling around, he glanced back at Cerise and True, who had both strapped themselves into the rear seats.

Tears streaked True's cheeks, which were mottled pink. "Captain?"

CHAPTER

FOUR

T rue clutched her hands in her lap to keep them from shaking as the transport ship burst out of the station and dodged enemy fire. What had just happened?

She stared at the back of his head as he sat in the copilot's chair, talking with the other Drexian officer. The one who'd called him captain.

He looked around, his ice-blue eyes locking on hers, and her cheeks heated.

"Captain?" she managed to ask, before the other Drexian said something to pull his attention back to their escape.

He hadn't answered her question yet, but that didn't stop True's mind from spinning. Captain of what? This ship? A battleship? The space station?

True gave her head a small shake, as if to dislodge the insanity of it all. Just a few minutes ago, she'd been happily standing on the shore of the Gulf of Mexico and letting the crystal-clear water lap at her toes. Sure, it had been a holographic ocean, but it had felt real. Just like he'd felt real when he'd grabbed her—ripping her from her peaceful moment—and told her they needed to go because the station was under attack.

At first, she'd been elated to see him. After all, she'd been waiting for him. Hoping he'd come strolling down the long stretch of white sand like he usually did and take her hand in his.

But this time, his hand hadn't been soft and warm, sending shivers down her spine as he ran it through her hair and traced one finger down her throat. No, this time his grip had been firm and insistent. And his expression had been all wrong. Usually, he was calm and quiet, listening to her talk while he held her in his strong arms. Smiling and laughing easily, the corners of his eyes crinkling.

Today, he'd been anything but calm. He'd practically screamed at her, and there was little trace of the sweet, searching expression she'd grown used to. No, this was someone entirely different. This man was dominant and imposing and clearly used to being in charge.

A chill went through her. She kept her eyes on his broad back, as if tracking a dangerous creature. Maybe Ella used this Captain Whomever as a model for the hologram she created. He *was* incredibly handsome, even if this version looked like he hadn't slept in days. He certainly hadn't shaved.

Red lights flashed on the console, illuminating the cockpit with a crimson glow. Both Drexians muttered low as they studied the readouts, but True felt like she was hearing everything from underwater. Their voices sounded muffled, and the words made no sense.

"Are you okay?" Cerise's small hand closed around hers.

True jerked her attention to the alien strapped into the chair next to hers, her feet dangling off the floor. The warmth of her hand was comforting, and True placed her hand on top of the Perogling's. "Fine."

"Mmhmm." Cerise eyed her, cocking her head to the side so that her wig slipped a bit. "You don't look fine. You look like you saw a phantasmor."

"A phantasmor?"

Cerise nodded. "You know, energy that's left its host body."

"A ghost?"

A shrug from the little alien. "If that's what you call them. There were plenty on Lymora III. Lots of restless spirits were released on that place, let me tell you." She fluttered her free hand. "Anyway, you look like you saw one, and then it slapped you."

True touched her fingertips to her hot cheeks. "I was startled, that's all." She motioned her head toward the two Drexians in front of them and dropped her voice. "Do you know the older guy?"

Cerise's heavily painted eyes widened. "The silver fox?" She made a purring noise in her throat that was surprisingly realistic. "Why, do you have dibs on him?"

The ship banked hard to one side, and True took her hand from under Cerise's, pressing it to the cool ebony wall for balance. She was glad she hadn't eaten breakfast, or it might be all over the shiny, curved walls of the cockpit by now. "No, of course not. I've never met him. At least, not the real him. I think I know a different version."

Cerise put a hand under True's elbow and squeezed.

True pulled away quickly. "What are you doing?"

"Checking to see if you're feverish. Why? Is that not how humans check for fever?"

True gave a small laugh in spite of herself. "Not exactly. And I don't have a fever."

Cerise eyed her as if she didn't believe her. "Then maybe you hit your head, sweetie, because you're not making any sense. How could you know a fake version of the Boat's captain?"

True's mouth went dry. The captain of the Boat? When they got to wherever they were going and met up with the rest of the residents of the space station, she was going to find Ella and kill her.

"I can't believe you did this," she muttered to herself, wishing she could be saying it to her best friend.

"Did what?"

True glanced up and saw Cerise's pinched face. She guessed she did sound crazy, mumbling about fake men. "Don't worry. I'm not crazy and I'm not seeing phanta...phantom...I'm not seeing ghosts. I think Ella used the captain as a model for a holographic guy she added to my simulation."

"Really?" Now the alien looked intrigued. "So you and the Captain have been engaging in a little holographic—?"

True shushed her, hoping the Drexians were too busy flying the ship and dealing with the various beeps and flashing lights to listen to them. "No, nothing like that. I don't even think you can do that with a hologram."

Cerise bobbed her head up and down vigorously. "Oh, yes, you can."

"Okay, then." True's warm cheeks reminded her that even talking about sex made her blush. "That wasn't what this was, though. Ella added him in so I could talk with him. She knows the Drexians intimidate me, so I think she put one in the program to help me get more comfortable."

"That's what she told you?"

"Not directly," True admitted. "I actually never got to talk to her about the guy she added. I assumed that's why."

Cerise nodded slowly, glancing from True to the captain and back again. "So you don't know for sure."

True followed her gaze, shifting in her chair as she watched the Drexian's large hands flying across the console. "Know what for sure?"

"That it wasn't really him in the holodeck."

True laughed—louder this time—and both Drexians glanced back quickly before a beeping sound drew them back to the console.

"That's ridiculous. Why would the captain of the Boat be in my holodeck simulation? He has no idea who I am. I'd never laid eyes on him outside the holodeck before ten minutes ago."

Cerise frowned, wrinkling her brow.

"Sorry, ten thrums ago." True always forgot that the alien measured time differently.

"Why would Ella put him in your program?"

It was a good question. Until now, True had thought her friend used what she knew of True's likes and dislikes when it came to men, although now that she thought about it, had she ever told her best friend that she had a secret fetish for left-handed men? Doubtful. It wasn't the kind of thing that popped up in conversation, although it was considerably less quirky than most fetishes. "I don't know. I guess because he's so..."

"Gorgeous?" Cerise finished her sentence for her with a whisper.

"Yeah." He *was* gorgeous, even if he wasn't a young buck like most of the Drexians she'd seen around the ship. She'd always thought the gray streaks in his dark hair made him look distinguished and sexy, and there was something steady and solid about him that drew her in. He wasn't impulsive and wild like a lot of the younger Drexians she'd heard about.

In all the time they'd spent together, he'd never tried to seduce her or move any faster than she'd wanted to go. He'd been content to kiss her on the sand, his hands never roving. There were times she might have thought about jumping on top of him, but he'd never pushed her. She'd always thought that patience came with age, but that in her case it was a setting installed by Ella. *Because I was just kissing a hologram,* she reminded herself.

She stared at his back, remembering running her hands across the muscles that now tensed as he worked. *Wasn't I?*

He spun around in his chair to face her. "Are you both okay?" He appeared to be asking both women, but his gaze never left True's.

She nodded, unable to speak. Just a hologram, she repeated in her head. *I've never met this guy before.*

"I know I have a lot of explaining to do," he said, leaning forward. "But I should introduce myself first. I'm Captain Varden."

This was good. He was holding out his hand for her to shake. Would he do that if he already knew her?

"True," she said, her voice cracking.

"I know." He smiled as he took her hand, stroking the back softly with his thumb, his touch sending an electric sensation up her arm.

26

She jerked her hand back, her mouth falling open. How would he know to do that if he wasn't...?

His smile faltered. "I promise to explain why I've been coming into your holodeck simulation as soon as I get you to safety."

True rubbed her hand where he'd held it, a scorching heat remaining from his touch. It *was* him. He'd been in her simulation. "It was actually you? Not a hologram?"

Tears stung the backs of her eyes. The actual captain of the space station had been the one she'd been kissing and dreaming about. She hadn't been sharing her most intimate thoughts with a holographic projection, she'd been confiding in a real Drexian. The captain of the fricking station had tricked her into thinking he was a fantasy so he could. . .what? Make out with her? Get in her pants eventually? The one guy she's thought had been completely harmless was actually a big, badass Drexian captain?

True put her head between her knees. Breakfast or no breakfast, she was definitely going to be sick.

CHAPTER
FIVE

Varden turned to face the console as a beeping noise grew louder, casting a final glance back at True with her head between her legs. Well, this wasn't good. Her mouth had gone slack when she'd realized it had been him with her in the holodeck the whole time, and now it looked like she was going to be sick.

He tried not to be too hurt, but it wasn't the reaction he'd been hoping for. What had he been hoping for? That she'd throw her arms around him and tell him she'd dreamed of him being real? Maybe, although now it appeared that he'd underestimated how shocked she'd be.

True clearly wasn't thrilled about him being real. Was she upset he hadn't told her the truth from the start, or was she embarrassed that she'd kissed him? She was probably half his age, he reminded himself. What might have seemed like harmless fun in the holodeck might not be something she'd want to admit outside of it.

He swallowed hard. Of course, it had been foolish to think that someone as young as her would be interested in him. Not when she could have her pick of Drexians. And now that she was meeting him face-to-face in the real world, she clearly wasn't impressed.

Varden didn't have too long to dwell on the mess he'd made or the swirling ball of regret roiling in his gut, since the lights flashing told him they were running low on fuel.

"Captain," his first officer said, tapping the indicator light. "It looks like—"

"I see it, Kos." Varden cut him off. He didn't want to let on to the women that they might be in trouble. Not after everything they'd already gone through. "Was the ship fueled up when we left?"

"Affirmative. Checked it myself." The officer tapped another blinking light and lowered his voice. "I think we got hit during our escape. Our hull took some fire."

Varden nodded grimly, watching the fuel levels dip even lower. "It's the only explanation for the sudden drop."

"We won't make it to the rendezvous point. And this ship hasn't been outfitted with jump technology yet."

Varden's ball of regret morphed into a hard pit of fear. He pulled up a star chart, his eyes scanning the sector for a habitable planet, preferably one with a colony. They'd left Earth's solar system behind—not that landing on Earth would have been a viable option —and now were far from the little blue planet. And, apparently, any colonized planets or moons.

"Nothing," Kos said.

Varden clenched his jaw as the fuel level continued to plummet. He touched a finger to a tiny green dot on the screen, enlarging it. "Nothing colonized, but this one looks habitable."

Kos swiped his hand across the console to get more readouts. "Acceptable oxygen levels for the humans. Extremely high H_2O content in the air. Heavy vegetation."

Varden recalled things he'd learned about Earth's environment. Since he'd been stationed in their solar system for a decade, he'd taken it upon himself to learn as much as he could about the planet that provided the Drexians their mates. "It's a rainforest."

Kos glanced over at him. "Sir?"

"Lots of plants and humidity in the air. It sounds like the rainforests on Earth. What's left of them."

Kos frowned. "I assume our options for fuel will be limited."

"Unless we can find deuterium down there," Varden said. "Send out a transmission on a secure channel letting our fellow Drexians know of our destination. If we're lucky, one of the other transports can swing back around before we've landed."

He stood and turned, remembering True when he saw that she'd sat back up. She wouldn't meet his eyes, so he focused on the Perogling, who stared up at him. "We're going to make a stop on a nearby planet. I'd advise you both to stay strapped in."

"Where are you going?" Cerise asked as he walked past her.

He didn't want to admit that he was going to see how much survival equipment was on board the old ship. "Checking our supplies."

Striding out of the cockpit, he walked through the center of the ship and down a short corridor lined with built-in cabinets with no handles. He pressed the bottom of one dull black cabinet door, and it popped open, revealing blankets and tarps, as well as a decent supply of dried rations. He let out a relieved breath as he pulled out a foil pouch of crispy padwump. At least the old ship had been stocked properly.

"So that's it?"

True's voice made him drop the shiny packet and jerk around quickly. "What's it?"

"We aren't going to talk about it?" Her voice was high and breathy, and she clenched her fists by her sides.

Varden felt the ship jerk and splutter. This was not the ideal time for him to try to explain, although if they didn't make it to the planet, it would be the only time. He reached a hand out to touch her arm. "True, it wasn't intentional."

She snatched her arm out of his reach. "Not intentional? So you accidentally kissed me? And touched me?" Her voice broke. "You didn't mean any of it?"

That wasn't what he'd meant at all. How had she spun his words around like that? "Of course I meant it. What was an accident was me being in the simulation in the first place."

She crossed her arms over her chest. "You accidentally overrode the lock on the holodeck doors? How does that happen?"

He tried not to let his eyes dip down to where her folded arms pushed up her cleavage, clearing his throat and looking down at his own feet. "I was curious to see what the Gulf of Mexico looked like."

She paused for so long that he returned his gaze to her face. "You snuck in to look at the ocean?"

He shrugged. "I had never seen one, or the substance you call sand."

The ship pitched to one side, and he caught her before she slammed into the wall. He felt the engines shifting and hoped that meant they were entering the planet's atmosphere.

Righting herself, True straightened but didn't shake off the hand holding her arm. "So you didn't come in for me?"

"Not at first," he said, feeling a tingle from contact with her soft skin. "But every other time was to see you."

She stepped back, and his hand fell away. "But you never told me who you were. You let me believe you were a hologram. All that time, you pretended to be someone you weren't."

"I never lied to you."

She let out a harsh laugh. "But you omitted the fact that you're *real* and the captain of the Boat. That's the same thing as lying."

Her accusation stung. She was right. It had been a lie to keep the truth from her. "What would you have done if I'd told you?"

She opened her mouth then closed it again, pink splotches reappearing on her cheeks. "What do you mean?"

He took a step closer. "What would you have done if I'd told you who I really was? Would you have given me a chance?"

She blinked hard, her eyes glistening. "I don't know."

"Who is lying now, True?" His voice was soft, but his words made her jerk back. "It seems like I am not the only one who was fooling themselves. You liked the safety of the fantasy, but the reality is not so appealing, is it?"

She jutted her chin up. "I don't know what you mean—"

The ship spluttered again, then the engines went dead. They were officially running on fumes.

He grabbed her by the arm and propelled her forward, his stomach churning. "Come on."

She pulled against him. "I wasn't done talking—"

"We're about to crash land on an alien jungle planet," he said, cutting her off. "I suggest you save your complaints until afterwards. If we survive."

She gasped, but she hurried along beside him without another word. As they entered the cockpit, Varden stopped breathing.

Kos was trying to keep the ship on a controlled descent, but the thick green foliage was rushing up at an alarming speed.

Grek. There wasn't time to strap themselves in. As the nose of the ship hit the tops of the canopy of trees, Varden threw True to the floor and covered her with his body. The impact was instantaneous and violent, the ship pitching and jerking as it crashed through the dense jungle.

Between the sounds of Cerise screaming and objects impacting the hull, Varden felt True trembling beneath him. She was on her back with her hands pressed to his chest and her face buried in his neck, her breaths warm and fast. He cradled her head with one hand to keep her skull from slamming into the floor as they were lifted up and dropped back down as the ship kept falling.

With a final hard thud, the vessel stilled and everything went quiet. Through the ringing in his ears, he could hear Cerise whimpering and Kos breathing heavily. Slowly, he began to feel shooting pains from where his hands and elbows had impacted the floor again and again.

Blinking a few times, he peered down to where True lay under him. She seemed unscathed, although her face was streaked with tears and her lower lip trembled. "Are you unhurt?"

She nodded, but she didn't push him away. Instead, she lifted a hand to touch his cheek. "You?"

Her soft caress made his pains vanish, but before he could say anything more—tell her how sorry he was, how much he cared for her, how desperately he wanted her—his first officer's voice jolted him back to reality.

"Captain, you need to see this."

CHAPTER

SIX

True dropped her hand from his face as he glanced up. Now that the ship had stopped falling, she could catch her breath and look around. Her pulse raced, but she couldn't be sure if it was completely from the crash landing. Having his huge body pressed against hers, and in some moments slammed against hers, had definitely contributed to the fluttering in her stomach.

Varden stood, pulling her up along with him. He held her steady, his large hands resting lightly on her hips, as he searched her eyes. "Are you sure nothing hurts?"

He was so close to her, she was surprised he couldn't hear the thudding of her heart. She shook her head. "Nothing. I promise."

He nodded, letting out a breath and pulling his hands back.

"Wait a second," she said, seeing the blood trickling down his scraped knuckles. "*You're* injured."

His gaze flitted to his hands, then away again. "It's nothing."

"It's from protecting me, isn't it?" she asked, noticing that both hands were bleeding and remembering that he'd cradled the back of her head during the crash. His knuckles must have taken the brunt of the impact.

He locked eyes with her for a moment, and her mouth went dry.

She knew there was no point in telling him he shouldn't have done it. Drexian warriors were all about honor, and she knew him well enough to know he didn't consider it a sacrifice. Before she could attempt to thank him, his first officer cleared his throat.

Varden held her eyes for a moment longer before leaving her to join the other Drexian.

True rubbed her palms down the front of her skirt and swiveled her head. Aside from flashing lights across the ship's console, the cockpit seemed undamaged. Cerise was still strapped into her seat, although her wig was more than a little askew.

"You okay?" she asked the alien, who still white-knuckled the armrests.

Cerise tore her gaze from the front of the ship to look at her. "I think so. That may have been the least fun I've ever had in a ship, and that includes the time I had to service a Dardrolian and his three appendages."

True tried not to think about what that even meant, although she knew the Perogling had been a pleasurer before coming to the Boat. "You want me to unhook you?"

"That depends. Are we still as high up as it looks?"

True's eyes followed the stubby finger Cerise pointed out the front of the ship. Her mouth fell open. Cerise was right. It looked like they weren't on the ground at all.

"Captain?" True asked, the title sounding strange coming from her mouth.

When he turned, his furrowed brow did not inspire confidence. He glanced at Cerise and her outstretched arm. "We seem to be lodged between two trees, but only about a metron off the ground."

"A metron?"

The corners of his mouth quirked up. "About four of your Earth meters."

"That's not so bad." She joined him at the front and peered out over the gunmetal gray nose of the ship. Just as he'd said, the ground looked to be a little over ten feet below.

It was hard to see where the thick leaves of the trees ended and the vegetation covering the ground began. Bright green vines hung down from the tall trees, wrapping around the thin trunks and pooling at the roots. She didn't see any creatures, but she felt sure they were out there.

"It makes it hard to leave," the first officer said, touching a hand to a red knot on his forehead. "We may not fall, but if we're wedged in here, there's no blasting off either."

"We'd need fuel to blast off," Varden said.

"So we're stuck here?" True didn't want to panic, but it seemed like they'd gone from bad to worse.

"Until the rescue arrives." The captain straightened, rubbing the scruff on his cheeks.

When he was at his full height, she was reminded of just how large he was. She could practically feel the heat radiating off his body as he stood next to her with his shoulders squared.

The blood streaking down the backs of his hands caught her eye, and she was glad for the distraction. Anything to take her mind off his size and closeness, and how much both gave her an unwanted thrill. "Why don't I go find the med kit?" When he started to protest, she waved a hand at his first officer's head. "For both of you."

She took long steps out of the cockpit and into the center of the ship, pausing when she realized she didn't know where to look. When she'd found him earlier, the captain had been looking in a wall cabinet down a short corridor.

True wasn't used to thinking of him as the captain. In her mind, he was still the hot hologram in the martial arts uniform. Although, if there was any question as to whether he was real or not, the crash landing put that to bed. There was no denying he was one hundred percent flesh and blood, and she'd gotten up close and personal with quite a bit of his flesh.

Her mind flashed back to his hard body pressed against hers, and then to the feel of his scruff as she'd stroked his cheek. She squeezed her eyes shut. What had gotten into her? If his first officer hadn't called out for him, True might just have kissed him.

She opened her eyes and gave herself a mental shake. This was not the time for fantasies, no matter how much she'd wanted to feel his lips against hers again. She was looking for the med kit, she reminded herself, quickly locating both the corridor and the inset cabinets. After a minute of prodding, she had the cabinet doors opened.

True pawed through the supplies. Some looked familiar, like blankets and clothing, while others looked unfamiliar—weapons and tech she was sure were way more sophisticated than anything on Earth. She avoided touching any of the tech for fear she'd blow her head off, but she grabbed a red box that looked promising.

Popping the latch, she peeked inside. Not everything looked like it would have belonged in a human first aid kit, but there was enough crossover to assure her she'd found what she was looking for.

"Bingo," she whispered as she closed it again.

"Bingo?" Cerise's voice made her nearly drop the med kit.

"How do you move so quietly in those shoes?" True asked, pointing to the platform shoes that reminded her of the ones worn by the Gatazoid wedding planner.

Cerise shrugged. "I learned to move quietly when I worked in the pleasure house. It paid not to wake the sleeping aliens."

True had never asked Cerise about her life before coming to the Boat, partly because she didn't want to know all the horrible things the alien had been forced to do. She took in the petite creature. "You sure you didn't get hurt during the crash? I found medical supplies."

"No. I was strapped in pretty well." Cerise gazed up at True and grinned. "But you had a bumpier ride."

"It was a little rough," she said, ignoring the woman's pointed look as she shut the cabinet and headed back toward the cockpit. "But the captain took most of the impact."

"I saw." Cerise ran to keep up. "He was holding you pretty

tightly. I wish I'd ridden out the crash being held by a big, gorgeous Drexian warrior."

True stopped in the middle of the ship. "It wasn't like that."

"No? That's too bad then, because I could light a Hexloid battle torch from the sparks coming off the two of you."

So much for keeping things under wraps. "Really?"

Cerise bobbed her head up and down. "He's hot. You're bothered. I've had holo-novels that are less dramatic."

"Whatever it was is over," True said, with more force than she felt. "Nothing can happen between us anymore."

"Why not? He's not tall, dark, and handsome enough for you?"

"That's not it. Of course that's not it. He's plenty tall, dark, and... It's just that I can't take a Drexian mate."

Cerise angled her head at True. "Because you're an independent? I think Ella and Shreya proved that theory wrong."

True twirled a strand of hair around her finger. "It's not that. The Drexians are all too..."

Cerise leaned forward, balancing on her toes. "Too?"

"Big," True whispered.

Cerise's eyes bugged out. "Do you mean their—?"

True clamped a hand over the tiny alien's mouth. "Yes. That and everything. It's just scary. Kissing him was nice, but I know he'll want more. All men do, right?"

Cerise shrugged and nodded, mumbling something beneath True's palm.

"I just don't think I can handle more. When he was a hologram, it was okay. It wasn't real. He wasn't real. A hologram doesn't have needs or want more than I can give. I know all the other women talk about how much fun it is, but I was always told that it wasn't supposed to be fun. It was supposed to be a duty.

Cerise pushed her hand aside. "A duty? Who told you that?"

"My parents."

Cerise eyed her, then gave a low whistle. "They did a number on you, didn't they?" She took True's hand and patted it. "Don't worry.

Leave it to me. I'll have you begging to have that man back on top of you in no time."

True shook her head. "Trust me, it's never going to happen. Whatever we had is done. The last thing I want is him on top of me again."

"We'll see," Cerise muttered, clomping off to the bridge.

H e stepped back, leaning against the curved wall of the cockpit. Well, that was pretty clear. The last thing she wanted was to be in close contact with him again.

He'd been on his way to look for True and help her locate the med kit when he'd caught the tail end of her conversation with Cerise. Actually, the last thing she'd said before the Perogling's footsteps had approached him, and he'd slunk back through the doorway.

Varden knew he shouldn't be surprised. It had been pretty clear how upset and startled she'd been by the news that he wasn't who she'd thought he was. Had he really expected things to go back to the way they'd been? Wished was more like it.

After the way she'd touched him after the crash, he'd held out hope that she'd forgiven him, that she could move on. Ideally, with him. He swallowed a hard knot of disappointment. Guess not.

Cerise entered the cockpit, glancing quickly up at him. He let her pass and drew back even further when True walked in.

She blushed when she saw him, holding up the med kit and looking away quickly. "Found it. Who wants to go first?"

Varden knew he couldn't take being touched by her right now.

Not when he knew how she felt. She didn't want to be close to him, and at the moment, the last thing he wanted was the torture of being near her. "Take care of Kos. I'm going to do some recon."

His first officer spun around. "Sir?"

"Since this ship isn't blasting out of here, we're going to need to leave it at some point. I'm going to assess the surface conditions and check out the damage to the hull."

True gaped at him. "You're leaving?"

He didn't meet her gaze. "You'll be perfectly safe with my first officer."

His words were clipped, and he regretted them as he saw her flinch. It didn't matter, he told himself. He was the captain, and he needed to do his job, no matter how much his heart ached.

"But your hands..." she argued, reaching for him.

He shrugged and moved them back before she could touch him. "I'm fine."

She dropped her arms and pressed her lips together. Both Cerise and Kos stared at them, the tension crackling in the air.

"I'll monitor you from here, Captain," Kos finally said.

"Good." Varden focused on his first officer, feeling a sense of order and calm settle over him as his brain automatically went through military procedure. "Keep an open channel in case we get a response to our last transmission. One of the other Drexian transports must have decrypted it by now."

"Yes, sir." Kos swung back to face the console.

Varden gave a final, cursory glance at the two women and strode out of the cockpit. This would be good, he thought, as he retrieved an environmental suit from one of the cabinets and pulled it on over his uniform. He needed to be doing something, so he wouldn't have time to think and regret.

The thin fabric shimmered as he fastened it, strapping a band to his wrist that shrunk to fit him like a second skin. Running a hand over the smooth surface, he watched it change color from the black of the surrounding walls to the bronze hue of his skin. This would come in handy when he was outside in the jungle. Not only would the suit protect him from heat or cold or any toxins in the air, it morphed color to match the surroundings, making the wearer virtually invisible.

As the captain of the Boat, he'd spent most of his time on the bridge. It was a job he loved, but he welcomed the chance to get back in the field. Or in this case, the jungle.

Varden strapped a blaster to his belt, slung a pack of emergency supplies over one shoulder, then pulled a curved blade off the wall. He smiled as the steel glinted. If he had a choice, he preferred the old Drexian methods of fighting over using the brute force of a blaster. He hooked the blade onto his waist. Hopefully, he would need neither.

When he was suited up, he returned to the center of the ship, where True stood with her arms folded tightly across her chest. He hesitated when he saw her.

"Is this smart?" she asked. "Leaving the ship?"

He bit back a flash of irritation. He wasn't used to being questioned. He certainly wasn't used to implications that his actions weren't smart.

"Yes," he said, pressing a code into a panel that opened a hatch on the ceiling.

"Yes?" She gave a choked laugh. "That's all I get?"

He closed the distance between them in a single stride until she had to tip her head back to look up at him. "What is it you want, True?"

She opened and closed her mouth, but nothing came out.

Looking down at the panic in her eyes, he shook his head. It was no use. She didn't look at him the same way, and he couldn't bear to see the brute she clearly thought he was reflected in her fearful expression. He backed away, lifting his arms up to grab the metal bars on either side of the hatch. "I'll return soon."

He hoisted himself up with a single motion until he was in the cramped compartment overhead. He fastened the hatch below him before flipping up the hood and facemask on his suit and popping open the hatch overhead.

The metal groaned as he pushed it up all the way and climbed out onto the roof of the ship. He sucked in a breath. The view from inside the cockpit did not do the planet justice.

They were indeed wedged between two trees, but what he couldn't see from inside was how high the trees reached. Varden craned his neck to see the tops of the willowy trunks. Far above him, the trees fanned out, spreading a spider web of interlaced branches and diaphanous leaves. Gold light shone through the canopy, dappling the dark hull of the ship and illuminating the ground in an uneven patchwork.

What was also undetectable from inside was the cacophony of sounds surrounding him. He was used to the whirring, mechanical noises of a ship, but these were different. The jungle seemed to sing —leaves rustling as wind moved them, wings flapping, something cawing.

He appraised the distance to the ground before sliding down onto one of the wings and then leaping down, landing in a crouch. The vines and leaves crunched beneath his boots as he cleared the ship, walking in front of the nose. The descent through the trees hadn't been kind to the old ship. The already-dull metal of the hull was now covered in gashes, with some bits sheared off, exposing the wiring underneath. Not good. At least it seemed to be securely wedged between the trees.

He made a complete circle of the ship before waving up. Pulling out his communication device, he clicked it on.

"Looks like we're stuck," he said into the handheld device.

"Affirmative," Kos replied, his voice crackling. "No unusual movements on the ship's scanners."

Varden saw Kos's face through the tinted glass, and the officer gave him the all-clear signal. At least his first officer wasn't picking up anything on the ship's sensors.

Scanning his surroundings, he reminded himself to stay alert.

This was still an alien planet, and although they hadn't picked up any signs of habitation or colonization, he didn't know what might be out there. Or if it was hostile.

Varden pulled his scanner from his belt, activating it as he headed away from the ship. He couldn't help noticing that his environmental suit had indeed morphed into a bright green that matched the surrounding foliage. When he held up his arm, it appeared to vanish into the background.

As he continued walking through the jungle, he ducked under hanging vines and sidestepped pools of iridescent green water with steam rising from the surface. He wiped off his clear face mask several times as water beaded on the surface. Although he knew the air was breathable, he also knew it would be like inhaling steam. For now, he preferred the blend of oxygen being pumped into his mask.

Varden took a deep breath. It was good to be out of the ship and away from True. He never could have imagined a time when he would be eager to leave her. For the past few weeks he'd thought of little else but her, anticipating their next meeting and imagining what she was doing. But that was before.

He pushed aside a curtain of green vines. Everything was different now, although neither of them had actually changed. He was still the same person he'd always been with her. Now she just knew his name and that he wasn't a hologram. He wasn't sure why that changed everything for her, but it did. For him, she was still the same beautiful, perfect female. The one he couldn't get out of his mind no matter how hard he tried.

His foot caught on a crawling root and he stumbled, cursing himself for losing concentration. A Drexian warrior couldn't afford to be distracted, he told himself.

His scanner began flashing, and he stopped, bending to inspect the dark sliver of metal at his feet. Part of his ship. He picked it up, then spotted another panel about a metron away. He tucked the second one under his arm and decided to head back to the ship.

"Located some of our hull," he said into his device. "Heading back."

"Copy that." The voice responding didn't belong to Kos. It sounded like True. Even hearing her voice for a moment sent all his blood rushing south.

Grek. He adjusted himself, flinching as his cock strained against the tight fabric of the suit. This would make for a comfortable walk back.

He tried to distract himself by taking in as much detail about the alien rainforest as he could. Aside from some unusually large butterfly-type creatures flying overhead and some oversized insects scuttling about on the ground, Varden hadn't spotted any significant life forms. At least nothing threatening.

Reversing his direction, he cut a path back the way he'd come. He spotted the dark hull in the distance, incongruous amid the vivid green surroundings. As he locked his gaze on it, he blinked hard. Had it just moved?

Impossible, he told himself. It had been jammed between those trees. He increased his pace, not bothering to keep his footfall quiet. Unless the trees themselves were falling from the weight.

He cut his eyes to the floor of the forest as his feet sank into something. When he looked up again, the ship had dipped even lower. Jerking his feet out of the pool of mud, he ran as fast as he could toward the ship, swatting branches out of his face.

When he reached the ship, he staggered back before falling into a widening pool of shimmering blue mud mixed with leaves and broken vines. One foot slipped in, and he had to jerk hard to keep it from being sucked under.

His heart hammered in is chest as he looked up at the ship that held True. It wasn't falling out of the trees. The trees were sinking into alien quicksand.

EIGHT

"Did he leave?" Cerise asked as True walked back into the cockpit.

She nodded, focusing on the view out of the front of the ship and trying not to think about the hurt look in his eyes before he'd disappeared through the hatch. Right after he'd asked her what she wanted, and she'd been rendered speechless.

What did she want? She wound a strand of hair around one finger until it was tight enough to pinch her scalp, then released it. She wanted for things to go back to the way they were, before she knew who he really was. She wanted the fantasy back.

She stepped up behind the first officer when she heard Varden's husky voice. He was below them, talking into a small device, although it was hard to make out his large form in the suit he was wearing. It was the same color as the foliage around him, making him look like a floating face.

After telling him their sensors weren't picking up anything unusual, Kos waved, while Varden turned and strode away. Her eyes tracked him until he'd vanished into the forest. Even then, she didn't look away, her stomach a tight ball of worry.

"I'd like one of those suits," Cerise said.

Kos rotated his chair. "An environmental suit?" He appraised the tiny woman. "They adjust to fit, but I'm not sure if they can shrink that much."

"I don't mind if it blouses."

The Drexian raised an eyebrow, and True suspected blousing wasn't what a suit designed for seven-foot-tall alien warriors would do on a tiny creature who barely reached True's waist.

The first officer looked between the women, his light-gray eyes narrowed. "You should both wear one in case we need to leave the ship for any reason. Protocol dictates we prepare for exposure."

"I'm all for protocol," Cerise said.

Kos sighed, glancing out the front of the ship, then at True. "Can you monitor the captain's transmissions while I get the suits?"

"Sure." She liked the idea of having something to do. Anything to take her mind off the fact that Varden was outside alone on an alien planet. "Do I have to press any buttons?"

"Only if you want to talk." He stood and waved her into the chair, pointing to a blue oval on the flat panel. "Tap that to respond. Otherwise, don't touch a thing."

She gave him a mock salute, but he didn't smile. Cerise, on the other hand, was grinning brightly.

"Got it," True said. "Don't touch anything."

After they'd left, she leaned forward, taking care not to rest her hands on the wide console. She had to admit, the planet was pretty. She knew it could be a lot worse.

She'd heard that the tribute bride Trista had been stranded with her mate Torven on a planet that was completely ice. She rubbed her bare arms just thinking about it. Growing up in the American South had given her thin blood. Anything below fifty degrees Fahrenheit made her reach for a sweater.

A few beads of water trickled down the glass overlooking the ship's nose. It looked steamy outside. True wondered if this planet had its own version of mosquitos. She wrinkled her nose. She hoped not, but she'd never been in a tropical climate that didn't have tons of biting insects.

That had been one nice thing about her Gulf of Mexico holodeck simulation. It had all the wonderful parts of the beach, with none of the irritating ones—no bugs, no crabs scuttling out of holes in the sand, and definitely no sharks.

Thinking about her beach simulation made her shoulders relax. She rested her head against the back of the pilot's chair and closed her eyes, letting her mind drift back to a memory of sitting on the sand, leaning back against him. His arms were wrapped around her, and the top of her head was tucked in underneath his chin. His breath was slow and steady, matching the rhythm of the waves as they rolled in and back out again.

Her eyes had been closed then, too, and she'd been keenly aware of the feel of his hard chest muscles against her back. She could feel his heart beating—not slow, like his breathing, but fast, as if he'd just run a race. Her own pulse fluttered as he rubbed his fingers down the bare skin of her arms, leaving what felt like scorch marks behind.

When she couldn't take the anticipation anymore, she'd turned and settled herself on his lap, wrapping her legs around his waist and watching the pupils of his blue eyes grow wide. Normally, True would never be brave enough to make a move like that. Deep down, a little warning voice told her she was acting like a slut, but she'd ignored it. She couldn't be behaving shamelessly, as her mother would have put it, if the guy wasn't even real.

She'd run her hands down his chest, savoring the feel of every rock-hard curve. He hadn't made a move, even though she could feel his body quivering. He'd waited for her to kiss him before circling his arms around her and pulling her into him.

The kiss had quickly gone from tentative to searching, and she'd moaned when he'd parted her lips with his tongue. The taste of him had been intoxicating, and she'd wanted more. When she'd rocked her body into his, she'd felt something big and hard.

The cloud of desire had cleared slightly as she realized just how big and how hard it was, her heart pounding as she felt it pressing against her. A traitorous pulse had throbbed between her legs, and she'd pulled back, breathless. His eyes had flashed as his strong hands held her to him even as she'd squirmed, her fear overtaking her desire. She'd been surprised by how aroused she'd been when he'd held her in place, her attempts to run thwarted by his strength. But he'd done nothing more. Just held her.

True opened her eyes. Her heart was pounding just like it had been then, and her palms were damp. She shifted in the chair. Her hands weren't the only wet thing, she thought, feeling a hot pulse between her legs and squeezing them together.

"Great," she whispered to herself. "It's not like I have a spare pair of panties."

How could Varden get her so hot when he wasn't even on the ship?

She peered out the front of the ship again. No sign of him, although her view seemed to be different. Unless her mind was playing tricks on her, they seemed to be lower.

"Located some of our hull." Varden's voice filled the cockpit. "Heading back."

She fumbled to locate the blue oval on the touch screen, finally touching it, then pausing as she wondered how to respond. Was there an official Drexian military response? Probably, but she didn't know it. She searched her memory, finally saying, "Copy that."

There was no response, so she turned her attention back to the fact that she was almost one hundred percent sure they were closer to the ground than they had been when she'd first sat down.

"What do you think?" Cerise asked from behind her.

Wrenching her gaze from the view, she swiveled to see the woman wearing one of the special suits, the arms and legs rolled up. The fabric was black and blended perfectly with the walls of the ship. Kos stood behind Cerise, also in a suit, but his fit him like a second skin. She'd been so distracted by fuming at Varden, she hadn't noticed before how big and hunky his first officer was. No surprise. She hadn't laid eyes on one who wasn't huge and gorgeous. And like all Drexians, Kos had dark hair and perfectly bronzed skin.

"Any word from the captain?" he asked as she stood to let him take his seat back.

"He's on his way back."

Kos handed her a bundle of dark fabric. "We brought one for you to put on."

"Thanks." She hesitated, not sure if she should tell him her theory that they were getting closer to the ground. It sounded a little crazy considering she hadn't felt the ship move.

He squinted as he looked outside. "Are we—?"

The ship lurched back before he could finish his thought. Okay, maybe her theory wasn't so crazy after all.

The sound of gasping breath filled the cockpit. It was Varden. "You've got to get out of there," he yelled. "The trees and the ship and everything around it are sinking!"

Kos leapt to his feet again, moving so fast True could barely catch her breath before he'd pulled them all out to the center of the ship. He pointed to the hatch she'd seen the captain go through earlier. "We can get out this way."

She still held the suit tight in her arms. "Should I put this on?"

"No time." He shook his head as the ship dropped a few feet and they all staggered to one side. "Take it with you and put it on once you've cleared the ship."

Kos grabbed her and hoisted her up without another word. She didn't even have time to worry that her short sundress was riding up and flashing him before she was pulling herself up through the hatch.

"Grab her hands and pull her up," he called up, thrusting Cerise into the air.

True grasped her friend's arms and pulled her up until both of them were crouching over the internal hatch. Kos jumped up, jerking himself up as the ship pitched to one side. He closed the bottom hatch and popped open the top one, helping both women out onto the hull before joining them.

Glancing down, True spotted Varden. He wasn't far, but he appeared to be standing on the edge of a blue pool. A pool they were quickly sinking into.

"Throw them," he yelled.

Without warning, Kos picked up Cerise and tossed her over the side. She landed squarely in Varden's arms, and her impact barely seemed to register as he deposited her onto the ground.

"Now True," he called out, waving his arms.

"Ready?" Kos asked, putting both hands on her hips and not waiting for a response.

Suddenly, she was in the air, with the ground rushing toward her incredibly fast. She felt her skirt flying up, the air buffeting her bare legs, and the environmental suit in her arms flying out of them, then Varden caught her. His hands slid up her legs, pushing the fabric of her dress up until it was bunched around her waist.

She was so close to him, she could feel his breath against her cheek as she slid down the length of his body, and he placed her gingerly on the ground. Just over his shoulder, she could see the bundle of fabric she'd been charged with bringing with her sinking into the water. So much for her environmental suit, although the air seemed fine. Hot and sticky, but breathable.

"Now, you," the captain yelled up to his first officer moments before the ship lurched backward, sending Kos spiraling off the back before it hit the water with a loud splash, disappearing below the churning blue surface.

"Kos!" Varden screamed as his first officer flew backward and out of sight. He watched in horror as the ground collapsed, taking the trees and ship with it into the expanding pool. The water, which had been a bright blue, now churned dark with loose soil and foliage.

He pulled True and Cerise back, his gut twisting as he stared slack-jawed at the spot where the transport had just been—now a swirling pond. Was his Drexian crew mate in there somewhere? He balled his hand into a fist. He couldn't let Kos drown. Not after the man had gotten both women out safely. Not after he'd saved True.

He cast a quick glance to where True knelt down next to Cerise, both women sobbing. "Stay away from the edge," he said before pulling up his face mask, grabbing the end of a thick vine, and diving into the water.

If he'd expected the water to be as warm as the air outside, he was wrong. The cold hit him hard, shocking his system, but he moved his limbs to warm them. Keeping one arm stretched out in front of him to feel for debris and the other grasping the vine—his lifeline back to the surface—he kicked down. His extended hand bumped into something hard—the top of the ship—and he used it to guide himself over and toward the back.

Even though everything had happened quickly, he felt sure Kos had landed somewhere behind the ship, so he groped wildly. Even though he could open his eyes, it didn't matter. The water was too filled with silt and debris to offer any visibility. Varden could breathe through his mask, but he suspected Kos didn't have much more time down below without air. The warrior had not had his face mask up when he'd gone over the back of the ship.

Thrusting his arm as deeply as he could, Varden's fingers brushed something that did not feel like part of the hull or a tree trunk. Hope fluttered in his chest as he wrapped his hand around Kos's arm, tugging the Drexian up. Crossing his arm over the officer's chest, he kicked up as hard as he could, pulling on the vine at the same time.

There was a hard jerk on the vine, and he cleared the surface. Varden looked up to see True and Cerise tugging on the vine and dragging him and Kos out of the water. When he reached the edge, he crawled out and pulled his officer behind him.

"Is he...?" True asked.

The Drexian wasn't breathing, but Varden refused to believe he was dead. He began pumping his chest. The forest seemed to have gone quiet as they huddled around the wet, limp body.

True leaned over, pinching Kos's nose and breathing into his mouth. Varden continued to press on his chest, mentally willing him to wake up. After another breath from True, Kos began to cough, spitting out a mouthful of water.

Varden rolled him over and pounded on his back until the Drexian held up a hand for him to stop.

"You did it." Cerise clapped as she bounced up and down. "You saved him."

He'd never felt such a complete sense of relief in his life. Everyone was safe. Leaning back, he looked up at True.

"You asshole," she said, practically spitting the words at him.

He tilted his head at her, unhooking the mask around his head and pushing it back. His universal translator implant was rarely mistaken, but had she just insulted him? "What?"

"You could have been killed," she said. "You could have been sucked under for good. You barely made it out of there alive. What were you thinking?"

Was he actually getting a lecture after saving his first officer's life? "I was thinking that I couldn't let Kos die."

"So you were willing to sacrifice yourself?" Her face blazed with fury.

What was wrong with her? Were all human females this irrational? He'd heard rumors that Dorn's courtship had been tumultuous, but he'd never heard of something like this. What had happened to the female who was shy and scared of her own shadow?

"I'm a Drexian warrior, so yes, I was willing to sacrifice myself for my crew mate. I would have done the same for you."

She stamped one foot. "I don't want you to save me."

"Well, that isn't something you get to decide." He was yelling almost as loudly as she was now, and both Kos and Cerise were gaping up at them.

Tears glittered in her eyes and her lower lip trembled, and Varden felt all the fight seep out of him. She wasn't angry, she was scared. He dragged a hand across his face. He was messing up again. "I'm sorry if I frightened you."

"You disappeared under the water and didn't come up for so long." Her voice sounded shaky, reminding him that she was young —much younger than him. She hadn't experienced battle or death or any of the things he'd seen when he was a younger warrior.

He pulled her into him, wrapping his arms around her and feeling her small body sag against his. "It's okay. We're all fine now."

He knew she was only letting him hold her because she was

shaking, probably from shock. As he stroked her hair, her breathing became more even.

"But for how long?" she asked.

"What?" He felt a twinge as she pulled back, missing the feel of her soft body as soon as she stepped away.

"We just lost our ship," she said.

He'd been so preoccupied with getting them all out of the ship and then saving Kos that he'd barely been able to process what had happened. She was right. Their only source of shelter and supplies now sat at the bottom of some sort of marshy sinkhole. All they had was what they were wearing and what was in the pack he'd taken with him. Not much for four people to survive on.

"The Drexian rescue party is probably already en route," he assured her with more confidence than he felt. "We might not even need to stay here overnight."

Kos pushed himself to his feet. His environmental suit was soaking wet, as was Varden's, and the steamy air was doing nothing to dry them. "Let's hope that second transmission got through."

"Second transmission?" He narrowed his eyes at his second-in-command.

Kos nodded, rubbing his temple, where he now had a second bump. "The first one failed because we were too close to a magnetic asteroid field. I sent a second one from the planet."

Varden's stomach did an uncomfortable flop. If neither transmission had been received, the Drexians would have no clue where to search for them. Especially with the ship and all its comms systems submerged underwater.

"Our people are excellent trackers," he said. "They'll find us."

This was true, although he didn't like the idea of waiting for a tracking party to locate them. Not that there was much he could do about it now. He saw that Kos and both females were looking at him for direction, so he threw back his shoulders.

"Kos and I will set up a shelter just in case the rescue party doesn't get here before nightfall." He glanced back at the water. "We should find more solid ground."

Kos nodded, swiping his dripping hair off his face. "Agreed."

"What should we do about them?" Cerise asked.

"Them?" Varden asked.

Cerise pointed over his shoulder, and he turned to see a cluster of small, wiry creatures with pale green skin holding what looked like very sharp spears.

CHAPTER
TEN

True rubbed her eyes, not sure if she was delirious or if she was, in fact, seeing little green aliens.

"No sudden moves," Varden said, his gaze sliding to his first officer as he raised his own hands into the air.

Kos looked unhappy with the order, but he obeyed and held his palms up. Cerise was the only one of them who didn't seem startled, and she gave the small creatures a finger wave. It struck True that the little green guys were around the Perogling's size.

Aside from being small, they had black hair tied into long braids that swung below their waists and swipes of dark paint underneath their eyes that extended up and out and gave a cat-eye effect. Long tails almost reached the ground, tipped with black like their hair and swinging next to the braids. It was easy to see that their bodies were lean and sinewy, since they wore nothing but some sort of animal hide around their waists. Not that True blamed them. It was too hot and humid on the planet to wear heavy clothing.

"We come in peace," Varden said, his tone even and calm.

One of the aliens cocked his head and responded with a string of words that True's universal translator mangled in her head. All she could understand was something about lightning.

Varden nodded. "That was our ship, but now it's gone." He pointed to the swampy sinkhole.

More chattering from the leader as the spears lowered. They were being invited somewhere.

"They want us to come to their village," Cerise said. "To a banquet."

"Are we the main course?" Varden whispered to her.

Cerise giggled, hiking up her soaking and sagging environmental suit. "Don't be silly. They're offering hospitality."

"Are you sure?" True was with Varden. The green aliens might be small, but she got the feeling they were good hunters and fighters. Their spears certainly looked sharp.

Cerise bobbed her head up and down. "Their language has the same root as mine. Who knows? We might even be distantly related."

From the little she'd heard about the Drexians being genetically compatible with humans, True knew that there was more of a connection between alien species throughout the universe than she ever would have originally guessed. She looked between the Perogling and these pint-sized creatures—one with pale blue skin and the others with green. It was definitely possible.

"Can they understand you?" Varden asked.

Cerise said something in what True assumed was her language, and the lead alien's face broke into a wide grin before he began chattering away at her.

"I think that's a yes," True told Varden.

Cerise walked toward the group, falling in step with them as they headed off through the jungle, the leader not pausing his chatter. After a moment, she stopped and looked back, beckoning at True and the Drexians. "Aren't you coming?"

True looked up at Varden. "Are we?"

She scooped his pack of supplies off the ground and hooked the strap over one shoulder. "They don't seem aggressive."

"You mean, aside from the weapons they pointed at us?" Kos muttered.

"We're the aliens here, remember?" Varden said, keeping his voice low as they moved along behind Cerise. "We're on *their* planet. We should attempt to keep things friendly."

Kos grunted, but he followed the captain.

"A captain and a diplomat," True said, slipping her hand into his and feeling instantly safer.

He looked down, closing his hand around hers. "It's my job to keep you safe, and this may be the best way to do that. We still don't know much about this place, so befriending the natives could keep us alive."

True shivered in spite of the heat, stepping closer to Varden. She knew she shouldn't hold his hand or encourage him in any way, but after thinking she'd lost him when he'd jumped into the water, she had an almost overpowering need to touch him and prove to herself that he was okay.

As they trudged through the dense foliage, she thought about how she'd reacted when he'd crawled out onto the bank, dripping water and dragging the limp body of his first officer. She'd never been as scared in her life as the moment she'd thought she might never see him again. Imagining him never returning from the treacherous waters had almost brought her to her knees.

She knew everyone thought she was timid and terrified of everything, but this was different. She'd lost people—her entire family when she was abducted, actually—but no one who made her feel like he did.

It was ridiculous, she told herself as she pushed a curtain of spindly vines away from her face. She barely even knew him. Not really. But the idea of losing him terrified her, and not just because they were stranded on an alien planet. He shifted her hand in his, and she felt a warm, tingling sensation radiating up her arm.

The heel of her sandal caught on a root and she tripped, nearly sprawling across the jungle floor before Varden caught her by the arm.

He looked down at her feet. "Have you been wearing those shoes all this time?"

She shrugged. They'd been fine when she'd been on the holodeck, although now they didn't seem like the best choice. "I didn't know I'd be crash landing in a rainforest. Next time you have plans to take me someplace like this, let me know, and I'll wear my jungle trekking outfit."

The corners of his mouth twitched, then he bent and scooped her into his arms.

"Hey! What are you doing?"

"You can't walk in those," he said. "You'll get hurt."

True felt ridiculous being carried like a baby, but she saw that her feet were already scratched from walking through the thick undergrowth. "Fine. As long as we agree that this isn't a usual thing. I'm perfectly capable of walking by myself."

"I would never suggest otherwise."

She narrowed her eyes at him, not knowing if he was mocking her or agreeing with her. Drexians were hard to decipher, and their sense of humor was very dry. He wasn't laughing, so she decided to take him at his word.

The motion of walking combined with the heat radiating from his body had a lulling effect on her, and soon she rested her cheek on his chest. Even through the fabric of his environmental suit and uniform, she could feel the hard planes of his muscles. As her eyes drooped, she traced a finger down the hollow of his throat, feeling the steady thrum of his pulse.

Everything about him felt so good. In her drowsy state, she wanted nothing more than to feel the solidness of him and the warmth of his big arms around her. She didn't care that he was a massive Drexian warrior who was huge everywhere.

All that mattered was that he was alive and with her and

keeping her safe. As she stroked the soft skin of his neck, she felt his breath become faster and could hear the thumping of his heart.

Then he was climbing, and leaves brushed her bare arms as they passed through thicker growth. She was only vaguely aware of seeing a latticework of treetop houses linked together by bridges made of vines. It looked like it stretched up as far as she could see, and she vaguely wondered how high Varden would have to climb carrying her. When she opened her eyes again, she was peering up at a green thatched roof.

She blinked a few times as she realized she was beneath him and his hand was brushing the bare skin of her thighs.

CHAPTER
ELEVEN

Varden tried to keep his mouth from falling open when the aliens stopped walking and pointed up. Instead of a traditional village with shelters on the ground, their houses were built into the canopy of trees, linking together with swinging vine bridges and topped with green thatched roofs. Small hammocks were tied between trunks, with platforms creating a winding, ladder-like structure that extended past where he could see.

The suns were setting, the fading light fighting to peek through low branches and dappling the ground. The temperature had not dropped, and rivulets of sweat trickled down his back and into the waistband of his pants.

He wished he'd pulled off his environmental suit earlier. It was clear he didn't need it for protection, as they all wore their hoods down, and True wasn't wearing one at all. Even though she wasn't heavy, carrying True had greatly increased his body heat. Just touching her made his pulse quicken, and holding her lithe body made his heart beat like he was being chased. When she'd started stroking his neck, he'd been afraid his knees would buckle.

Luckily, Kos had walked on ahead, so he couldn't see the bulge in Varden's pants. Try as he might, he hadn't been able to get it to go down. Not while she was touching him, her fingers featherlight along the hollow of his throat.

"Can you climb with her?" Cerise asked as the aliens began scrambling up the ladders and swinging themselves onto platforms.

The better question was, could he climb with a hard-on? Varden tipped his head back. "How far?"

The leader of the aliens chattered something about one tree, pointing up.

"Just up there," Cerise said, indicating the closest platform to the ground, although considerably over Varden's head.

"Fine," he said with a grunt, feeling True stir in his arms. He glanced at Kos, who shook his head.

"I'll stay down here."

The Perogling seemed to have no problem climbing up, and he saw her swinging in a hammock overhead that looked like it was made for her.

Tucking True into his chest, Varden hoisted himself—and her—up a few rungs of a ladder, ending up on a partially covered platform. The aliens on the planet weren't much into furniture, so there was nothing but a woven mat on the floor and what appeared to be a swinging chair. A wall of thin tree trunks bound together ran behind the floor mat, which he hoped would prevent True from rolling off.

Bending to fit under the thatched ceiling, he lowered her to the floor and deposited her on the mat. The roof was so low, he had to crouch over her, brushing a strand of pale, damp hair off her forehead.

She was so pretty and small, she took his breath away. Even sweaty, with her hair plastered to her face, she was the prettiest female he'd ever seen. His gaze traveled down to the soft skin barely covered by her slip of a dress. The skirt had ridden up when he'd carried her and set her down, so now most of her lean legs were exposed. He could even see a sliver of her pink panties.

Varden groaned and readjusted himself, tearing his eyes away.

What was he doing? They were stranded on a strange planet with a tribe of primitive aliens, and he was thinking how silky the fabric of her panties looked.

Grek. You're the captain of a space station, not a young Drexian who's never been with a female.

Like most Drexians, he'd visited the pleasure planets and enjoyed the affections of quite a few alien women. Although it had been a while since his last leave, he shouldn't be acting as if he'd never seen a scantily clad female before.

He gently pulled her dress down to cover her thighs, his fingers skimming across her skin. Her eyes flew open, fluttering as they focused, first on the surroundings and then on his face.

"What are you doing?" she asked.

He cleared his throat and tried to stand, but his head bumped the ceiling. "We're in the alien village. I was putting you down so you could sleep."

Her gaze flitted to her legs, and she tugged her dress even lower. "You weren't trying to...?"

Heat rushed to his face. "No. I would never force myself on you." His heart hammered in his chest as he thought about the accusation. Did she really think that of him? That he had no honor? That he would force himself on her while she was asleep? "You should know that."

Now her face reddened. "It's not like I've known you for a long time."

"You have known me long enough to know that. Have I ever touched you when you did not want me to?"

She sucked in a breath, then shook her head.

"I may have been afraid to tell you who I was, but I am still a Drexian warrior, and I still have honor. I would never claim a female unless she wanted me."

At the word "claim," she flinched. "Sorry. It's not like I know a lot of Drexians. All I know is that all men are after one thing. I guess

I figured Drexians are the same way. I mean, you look a lot like humans."

Anger flared inside him. Was this really what she thought of him? Of all males? Of all Drexians?

"If I only cared about one thing, I could have easily taken it already." He raked his gaze down her body. "No, True. The only way I will ever claim you for my own is if you ask me."

He saw her swallow hard. "Ask you?"

He nodded, then braced his hands on either side of her face and leaned down so that his lips buzzed her ear. "Ask me to fuck you."

She inhaled sharply, and he felt her body jerk. Standing with as much dignity as he could manage hunched over, he stomped off the platform and slid down the nearest ladder to the ground.

Ignoring the curious look from his first officer, he stormed off into the forest.

Idiot. Why had he said those things? If he'd wanted to convince her he was harmless and worth trusting, he'd just messed that up. Now she wouldn't be able to look at him.

He slammed his palm against a tree trunk. *Why had he lost his cool?*

Well, she'd insulted him, for one. The implication that he would ever force himself on any female had made him bristle. He may not be as young as he once was, but he was still a Drexian warrior and considered desirable by many. He knew that by the way some of the female aliens on the Boat had watched him. He didn't have to go to a pleasure planet to have females willing to spread their legs for him, although he preferred the no-string-attached arrangement of the pleasurers.

In all the hours they'd spent together on the holodeck, he'd never once been forceful. Actually, she'd been the one to kiss him first. She'd also been the one to climb onto his lap on the beach and straddle him. He hadn't initiated any of that, and now she was accusing him of trying something while she wasn't even conscious. He felt his ire growing again, but something else. Hurt. He was hurt that she would think this of him. He felt like he knew her, but she clearly didn't know him at all.

Because you lied about who you were, he told himself.

He growled and pounded his fist on the tree, startling a flat insect with a shiny blue shell, who scuttled up the tree and away from him. Maybe that mistake was something she'd never get past. He had to accept the possibility that he'd ruined his chance of a future with True. He never should have said what he did, but the woman made him crazy.

He leaned both hands against the tree and let his head dangle. Was that what he wanted? A future with her? He gave his head a quick shake. Even if she didn't feel like he'd betrayed her, did a Drexian as seasoned as him really stand a chance with a human so young and pretty? Did she even see him in that way, or had she just been using him for what she'd probably considered safe practice?

Swiping the back of his hand across his sweaty brow, he tapped the band on his wrist, and his environmental suit loosened. He pulled it off and balled up the fabric, resisting the urge to throw it as far as he could.

If only it wasn't so hot and sticky.

After years aboard the climate-controlled space station, the heat felt oppressive. And even though it was starting to be dusk, it wasn't getting any cooler. *Grekking hell.* He unbuttoned his uniform shirt, fanning himself with the loose fabric. He understood why the natives wore little more than loincloths.

Varden leaned against the trunk of a tree, blinking as the jungle around him darkened and the leaves began to glow. The rainforest that had been so bright green in the daylight now seemed equally as green in the dark, the plants giving off a photoluminescence that took his breath away. He touched a wide, fan-shaped leaf and it shimmered under his fingertips, the color morphing blue where he'd touched it and then going back to green. *Amazing,* he thought. And lucky for him, since he hadn't thought to bring any sort of light when he'd stormed away from the village.

Heaving in a deep breath, Varden straightened. It was time to apologize to True.

Walking back the way he had come, he kept his eyes up, using the glowing foliage for illumination, even as his feet fumbled across jutting roots. Where was the village? Hadn't it only been a few metrons away?

"Oof!"

He glanced down at the object he'd just kicked. Kos.

The officer jumped to his feet. "I was just resting my eyes, Captain."

"Where are the women?" Varden asked, his first officer's face a green glow in the light of the jungle.

Kos leaned his head back. Varden followed his gaze, squinting at the outlines of the hammocks and platforms—easier to spot because they weren't glowing green—as well as the creatures climbing and swinging throughout the vertical village. Now that he focused on the sounds, he realized the buzz of noise wasn't coming from insects or animals. It was the chatter of the natives as they talked in low tones above him.

"Either they don't need fire because of all this," Kos said, waving at the luminescent jungle, "or they haven't figured it out yet."

Since this was definitely a pre-industrial society, it could be either, thought Varden.

"It might not be wise to sleep on the ground," he told Kos. There had to be a reason the natives lived in trees, and he didn't want to find out why the hard way.

Kos instinctively glanced at his feet, then around the thick vegetation covering the ground. "Yes, sir."

The young Drexian climbed arm over arm up a nearby ladder until he reached an uncovered platform lodged between two trees, where he sat on the edge with his feet extending below him. "I'll keep first watch if you want to sleep."

Varden didn't feel like sleeping, but he did have something he wanted to do. "Agreed."

He couldn't help smiling as he studied the shadowy outline of the Drexian with his arms crossed over his chest as he systematically scanned the jungle. If he had to be stranded on a *grekking* hot planet, he was glad he was stranded with Kos. Not only had the warrior shown his loyalty by waiting for him with the last ship, but he'd saved True and Cerise from the sinking ship, almost losing his life in the process.

Varden was thinking about his brave first officer as he climbed up the ladder to the platform where he'd left True. Even though there was no light in the shelter, he could tell instantly that she wasn't on the mat. His heart hitched in his chest. Where was she?

CHAPTER
TWELVE

rue stumbled through the jungle. She'd been so hot and bothered when Varden had left that she'd needed to clear her head. Her plan was to walk off whatever feelings were making her heart race and her panties wet, but she'd gotten turned around. All the trees looked the same, and she couldn't see little aliens up in any of them.

Do not cry, she ordered herself as tears stung the backs of her eyes and threatened to fall. She couldn't be far. She'd only been walking for a few minutes. In one direction, that was. She'd reversed course a few times, so now the village could be anywhere.

The glowing greenery had been a surprise, and one that hadn't helped her orientation. It was even harder to make out shapes now that everything looked like it was the result of a radiation experiment gone wrong. If she wasn't so freaked out about being lost, she knew she would have thought it was beautiful.

She should call out. She was sure Varden would hear her and come running. *And think I'm a helpless idiot,* she thought. The last thing she wanted was the captain of the Boat to know just how clueless and inexperienced she was. He was so commanding and competent and seemed to know what to do in every situation, while she felt like she'd been bumbling through the entire day.

As she flashed back to what he'd whispered to her before he left, she felt a rush of heat between her legs. Even though it had shocked her, it had also ignited a slow burn in her core. His words had been so forceful and confident that she'd had to bite her bottom lip to keep from begging him to do it, to fuck her right then and there.

Even saying the word in her head felt scandalous, but a part of her loved the way it made her feel. She wished she was the kind of woman who could tell a man to fuck her, but even imagining it made her cringe. She could never pull that off, as much as she wanted to. If that's what Varden wanted—a woman who could beg him to fuck her—then she definitely wasn't that.

She shook her head, looking up again. The light coming through the tree canopy now was from what appeared to be three small moons, one glowing blue and the others almost yellow. None of them were as bright or big as Earth's moon, but their light bounced off the glowing greenery. Before she could pick a new direction to try, she heard the snap of a nearby branch.

Her pulse quickened as she froze. True had no idea what other creatures inhabited the planet or if they were friendly. Another snap, and then a heavy exhalation of breath.

True gave up being cool or trying to get back without Varden knowing she'd been lost. She screamed as she ran as fast as she could away from the noise. She felt her arms and legs being scraped and the fabric of her dress pulling as it snagged on sharp branches, but she didn't stop. Even when she heard the fabric tear and felt it flapping loosely against one leg, she kept running.

Something was behind her, breathing heavily and catching up quickly. With her arms in front of her to push away branches, True swallowed her sobs as she barreled through the jungle.

"True!" His voice made her stop suddenly, and he plowed into her, almost knocking them both to the ground.

He clutched her by the arms, holding her in front of him as he scanned her up and down. "Are you okay?"

"Something was chasing me," she managed to say.

"That something was me. I've been looking for you." He gave her a gentle shake. "Why did you leave the village?"

No way was she going to tell him she left because he got her too horny to sit still. "I just needed some fresh air."

"Well, you're not going to get it here. We're in a swamp."

She choked back a laugh.

"Oh, good! You found her." Cerise stood behind Varden with one of the aliens.

"I found her." He dropped one hand but kept hold of one of her arms, as if he thought she might try to run off again.

"What happened to your clothes?" Cerise asked, and True realized the small alien no longer wore the Drexian suit over her clothes, and the brightly colored outfit was now smudged and wrinkled.

Varden looked down at her, and she could see his mouth gape open. Glancing down, True realized that her dress had been shredded as she'd run through the trees and vegetation. It hung open, exposing everything from her waist down.

He cleared his throat as he shrugged off his own shirt. "Here. Wear this."

She gratefully took the shirt, glad he was so big that it was almost as long as her dress. Her hands shook as she buttoned it up, then her mouth went dry when she looked up and saw his bare chest. Holy cow, he was built. Not only were his chest muscles huge, his stomach was a series of hard bumps without an ounce of fat on them. It was so humid, his bare skin gleamed in the photoluminescence. She jerked her gaze away and tried to look anywhere but the gorgeous half-naked Drexian in front of her.

The native alien said something before pivoting and walking away. Cerise waved for them to follow. "Come on. Hopefully, the others are back at the village."

"Others?" True asked, falling in step with Varden.

"I sent Kos and some of the natives out to look for you, as well."

True's face burned, and she was glad the green light covered up her humiliated flush at having caused so much trouble. "I didn't mean to get lost," she said, regretting the words and the slightly petulant tone the moment she'd said it.

"It's okay. It's easy to get lost around here." He didn't seem upset now, although he'd been practically shaking when he'd found her. As they walked, he relaxed his grip on her arm. "I wanted to apologize."

She heard rustling overhead and realized they were back at the treetop village. She paused at the base of a ladder. "You don't need to apologize to me. I'm the one who owes you an apology. I know you would never...well, you know."

He took her hands in his. "Because you know me, True."

"I guess so." Part of her wanted to stay mad at him for tricking her for so long, but a bigger part of her felt like that had been a life-time ago. At least, it seemed like a million more traumatic things had happened since that morning, when she'd found out the truth about him. It seemed ridiculous to stay angry when they were each only one of four residents of the Boat stranded on an alien planet together.

She took a long breath. "I still don't think tricking me was cool, but I don't want things to be weird between us anymore. How about we start over?"

"Start over?"

"Pretend like we didn't meet before today and none of the stuff on the holodeck ever happened," she explained. "We wipe the slate clean and get a fresh start."

"Wipe the slate clean?"

"An Earth expression," she said. "What do you think?"

"If that is what you want."

"Good," she said, trying to make her voice sound bright. It was hard to see his expression in the odd glow, but he didn't appear to be smiling. She gestured to the platform above her. "I guess I'll get some sleep."

He took a small step back and gave her a slight bow. "Good night, then."

As he turned and climbed up a nearby ladder, she saw the bumps running down his spine. She'd heard the tribute brides— and even her independent friends Ella and Shreya—talk about Drexian nodes enough to know what they were immediately. She knew that they got hard and hot when the Drexians got hot and, well, hard. Seeing them for the first time in person made her want to touch them. Her fingers tingled as she imagined running her hands down his back and feeling his nodes harden under her touch.

He turned when he'd reached the low platform, catching her eye and making her look away. She hurriedly climbed her ladder and flopped down on the mat, lying on her back and staring up at the roof.

No way would she be able to drop off to sleep now. Not with her mind swirling with images of a shirtless Varden and his nodes. Feeling her nipples harden, True crossed her arms over her chest. That was no help. His shirt even smelled like him—spicy and masculine—and she raised the collar to her nose and inhaled deeply.

A shiver slid down her spine as she thought of him, remembering his kisses and realizing that, as scared as she was of his sheer size and her body's own traitorous reaction to him, she wanted more from him. Much more.

THIRTEEN

"Captain?"

Kos's voice stirred him from his sleep, and he shifted on the hard platform. Looking down, he saw his first officer on the ground. The warrior had stripped down to his uniform pants, as well, and despite the fact that slats of light barely peeked through the trees, the green glow of nighttime was gone, and the air was already hot and muggy.

Varden twisted his back to rid it of the ache from sitting up all night. The trunk of the narrow tree had not been the most comfortable thing to lean against, but at least he'd been off the ground. Aside from hearing the occasional flap of a wing during the night, he'd been surprised that no insects had bothered him. He'd been to planets where sand flies made breathing without a mask impossible, so he was grateful they'd landed on a planet without such creatures. The verdict was still out, however, on whether the planet was safe, he thought. It had already devoured their ship.

"Early riser?" he asked, sliding down the ladder and joining his first officer on the ground.

The Drexian shrugged. "Habit from the academy I never lost."

Varden nodded. Kos was such a dedicated and skilled officer, it was easy to forget he hadn't been out of the academy for more than a few years. "You sleep at all?"

Kos shrugged one shoulder. "Enough. I didn't want to miss the arrival of a Drexian rescue ship if it came in the night."

Another reason the warrior had risen in the ranks so fast and become his first officer. "And?"

A grim shake of the head from Kos. "Nothing. I'm concerned our transmissions did not reach our Drexian brothers."

Varden had the same worry, although he did not want to admit it to Kos. He clapped the officer on his bare shoulder, feeling the skin already slick with sweat. "Do not forget what skilled trackers we are. Especially Inferno Force."

Kos glanced up at the aliens moving easily between platforms and gliding down trunks and ladders, using their tails for balance or an extra grip. There was already a low hum of chatter as the village woke. "We cannot stay here indefinitely. We don't know anything about this species."

"Agreed. For now they seem friendly." He peered up and saw Cerise sitting on a high platform with a cluster of the aliens around her, seemingly inspecting her wig. Aside from the towering pile of curls, her pink suit made her look quite out of place among the barely dressed natives.

"Who knew the Perogling would make such a good ambassador?"

Varden cracked a smile. "Indeed. Let's hope she keeps us in their good graces until we can be rescued."

Kos rocked back on his heels. "I was thinking about returning to our ship."

"Returning? Our ship is underwater, or don't you remember being pulled under with it?"

The officer's cheeks colored, and he cleared his throat. "I remember, and I don't think I ever thanked you for—"

Varden cut him off with a wave of his hand. "There is nothing to thank me for. You would have done the same for me."

Kos gave a curt nod. "Yes, sir."

"Is your plan to get inside the ship or just revisit the site where it went down?"

Kos wiped a hand across his damp forehead, catching a few drops of sweat before they dripped into his eyes. "I'd hoped to get inside and make sure the beacon is still transmitting. I closed both hatches when we abandoned ship, so the ship shouldn't have flooded."

Varden rocked back on the heels of his boots as he considered the warrior's plan. If he had to be honest, it was exactly what he would have wanted to do when he was a young officer. It was risky, with a questionable chance of success. But it was also their only play.

They didn't have any other means of communicating with their people or letting them know where they'd landed. With their ship submerged, almost every bit of tech they had was underwater, as well. Even though Drexians were expert trackers, he wouldn't mind giving them as many clues as possible.

"All right," he finally said. "We'll go back to the ship."

Kos grinned, his gray eyes shining with pleasure. "Thank you, sir."

Varden looked up at the thatched platform where True slept. There were no signs that she was waking. What was there to say even if she had been awake?

She'd asked him to forget about everything that had happened between them before yesterday. A fresh start, she'd called it. Hearing her say that had been a punch to his gut. She was so ashamed of what she'd done with him that she wanted to pretend it had never even happened. Erase all trace of him from her past.

He'd agreed to it, of course. What else could he do? But the thought of wiping away all his memories of her was inconceivable. As painful as they were now that he knew she was embarrassed by them—embarrassed to have been involved with him—he couldn't sweep them away so easily.

His pulse quickened as unwanted thoughts of her filled his mind. He tried to push them away, telling himself that she wasn't interested. Not anymore. At least not in the real him. The best thing he could do was to focus on getting them off the planet. Once they weren't in constant contact, it would be easier to do what she'd asked. It would be easier to forget her.

"Captain?"

Varden jerked his attention back to Kos. "We might as well set out now." He located his pack on the ground and knelt in front of it, pawing through the contents until he found what he needed. He held up the long tube.

"Luminescence?"

Varden dug further into the bag, pulling out two foil packs and tossing one up to Kos. "That's breakfast." He held up the luminescence. "And this is to mark our path, so we can find our way back."

Kos grinned as he tore open his pack and lowered his nose, breathing in deeply. "I never thought I'd be so happy to smell fried padwump skin."

Varden hooked the pack over one shoulder as he stood. "Let's hope we get out of here soon. I don't have much more of that, and I suspect the natives don't have the same palates we do."

Taking a final glance up at the place where True slept, he pulled out his communication device and held it out as he led the way through the jungle. The ship was still emitting a communications signal. That was good. It was faint, however, which was not so good. If it was weak here on the surface, it would never be strong enough to break through the atmosphere and be detected by their ships.

At least he could use it to trace their way back to the ship. He couldn't tell the difference between one section of the jungle and another. To him, it was all tall willowy trees draped with vines and thick undergrowth. Every few steps, he dabbed a bit of glowing luminescence on a leaf or tree trunk at eye level. It would do them no good at night, but it should be effective during the day.

Kos threw an arm out to stop him. Varden looked down and saw that the ground ahead of them had turned to blue mud. No doubt the beginnings of the swampy sinkhole that had swallowed their ship.

They edged around the wide pond until they found a solid clearing, the air around the pool emitting a loamy scent. Surprisingly, the top of the ship now poked out from the surface of the water, the gunmetal-gray hull a sharp contrast to the blue water. One of the tree trunks also protruded from the pool, stretching across and resting on the far bank. It appeared that the water, which had been so filled with debris, was now calm—the branches and soil settled on the bottom.

"I think I can get to the hatch from that fallen tree," Kos said, before Varden could suggest he do that same thing.

"Let me go," he said, shrugging off his pack.

Kos was already busy unlacing his boots. "We've already determined that you excel in getting me out of the water, sir."

Varden fought a grin. "Are you being insubordinate, First Officer Kos?"

"Absolutely not, Captain," the Drexian replied, giving him a chest salute and a quick, crooked smile. "Just stating the obvious."

"I'll let you go first, but only because this mission was your idea. You should get the chance to see it through. Once you're in, though, I'm joining you."

"Yes, sir." Varden watched as the broad-shouldered Drexian took a short running start and leapt onto the tree trunk protruding from the water. The trunk dipped down, but Kos quickly scrambled up it and was soon making the short jump onto the top of the ship. The hull itself didn't shift, leading Varden to believe that it was resting on the bottom or on something solid enough to keep it in place.

Kos wrenched open the top hatch, then raised his fist in the air and called down, "The seal held!"

Varden felt a flutter of hope in his chest as he followed the lead of his first officer, leaping onto the tree trunk and running along the length until he could jump onto the hull. Climbing up to the hatch, he joined Kos in crouching low over the round opening. "After you."

Kos dropped down into the first locked compartment, then unlatched the second hatch and disappeared into the ship. Varden did the same, landing with a hard thud on the metal floor. The only light came from the now open hatches, the soft beam creating a cylinder of illumination in the dark interior.

He straightened and did a quick mental inventory. Miraculously, the inside of the ship was unscathed. The seals of the ship had held, and the emergency flaps that closed all vents had activated and done their job. None of the sludgy water had leaked inside.

He activated the light on his communication device and followed Kos into the cockpit, shining the beam in front of him. The Drexian stood hunched over the controls, his shoulder muscles bunched. Despite the pristine condition of the inside of the ship, there were no lights. No ambient or emergency lighting. No flashing alerts on the flat console. Nothing.

Varden squinted to look out the front, but all he could see was murky blue water. At least he didn't spot anything swimming around them. The last thing they needed was some horrific swamp creature to rise up from the depths. He shuddered at the thought and rubbed the now-bumpy flesh on his bare arms.

"*Grek* me," Kos mumbled, then glanced back and cringed. "Sorry, Captain."

Varden grinned. This was the first time he'd gotten a glimpse of his second-in-command out of his official role and not completely buttoned up on the bridge. A part of him liked this less formal version. "Not to worry. I agree with the sentiment. We are seriously *grekked*."

Kos let out a small laugh. "Yes, sir." He flipped levers and pressed buttons until finally there was a low hum and the console spluttered to life. His fingers flew across the dim illumination of the flat screen.

"Well?"

"It looks like my last transmission did get through," Kos said. "But it also appears our homing beacon has been damaged. It's not responding to commands."

"Can we set up a looping SOS transmission?"

Kos tapped the flickering console several more times before slamming the heel of his hand onto the edge. "Negative. The water may not have gotten inside the ship, but it appears to have damaged the wiring. Our comms aren't responding."

"Keep trying," Varden said. "It may just take a while for the systems to connect again."

Before Kos could respond, the ship groaned and the cockpit tilted forward. Varden grabbed the back of the pilot's chair to keep from slamming into his first officer, and as he looked out the front glass he saw that they were sliding down, nose first. His blood went cold when he heard the sound of splashing, and water rushed in around his feet.

Kos turned to him, his eyes wide as they both heard the sound of water pouring in through the open hatches.

"Belay that order," Varden said, grabbing Kos's arm and pulling him toward the only exit on the rapidly filling ship.

FOURTEEN

T rue rolled over and felt her nose bump against something hard. "Ouch."

Rolling away from the wall of tree branches bound tightly together, she sat up and looked out over the jungle. The vertical alien community was abuzz with activity and sound—the chattering of their alien language her universal translator couldn't quite decipher, the sound of feet scampering across wood, and flashes of green as they slid down ladders and across swinging vine bridges.

Even though they looked humanoid—although much smaller and with green skin and tails—they were a far cry from the other aliens she'd grown accustomed to on the Boat. The Neebix might have tails and small, nubby horns, but they were also the size of Earthlings and not green. The Vexlings were taller than humans, but their pale gray skin looked almost humanoid at times. It would have been hard to argue that the Gatazoids—with their small stature and hair that flushed pink when they were upset or agitated —looked human, but she supposed she'd gotten used to them. And they didn't prance around in loincloths. Then there were the Drexians. She sighed as she thought about the big, gorgeous aliens—and one in particular.

True didn't remember falling asleep—she never did—but she did remember why she tossed and turned so much before she drifted off. Varden. The sight of him in nothing more than pants, his chest and rippled stomach glistening, had been enough to make her forget to breathe. It didn't help that she'd slept in his shirt, breathing in his scent all night. And even though her dreams were hazy—the memory of them slipping away like sand through her fingers—she knew he'd been in them.

She raised the collar of his shirt to her nose and inhaled, sending a rush of pleasure through her body. Talk about a wake-up call.

"You're up!" Cerise's head appeared wig-first from around the other wall.

True dropped the collar, hoping the other woman hadn't noticed her sniffing it. "I'm up."

"I brought you breakfast." Cerise joined her on the platform, sitting down cross-legged and handing her a wide leaf filled with something bright orange and mushy.

True tried to muster a smile. "Thanks." She eyed the leaf without touching the contents. "What is it?"

"The locals call it flafaya." Cerise held up her own leaf and took a bite. "It's a fruit they pick from the very tops of the trees."

"Sounds like papaya," True said. "Does it taste like it?"

"What's papaya?"

True reminded herself that Cerise hadn't tasted most Earth food. "Never mind." She took a nibble of the sticky fruit, flinching from the sour kick. "So not like a papaya."

"It grows on you," Cerise said, putting her hand under True's leaf and lifting it toward her mouth. "Trust me. After a few bites, it will taste sweet."

True reluctantly took a few more bites, swallowing the fruit and bracing herself for the urge to pucker her mouth. It didn't come.

Cerise was right. The strange, gooey fruit became sweet after about the third bite.

"Not bad." She quickly ate what was in the leaf, realizing that she hadn't eaten for most of the previous day. It had been so crazy she'd barely noticed, but now her stomach welcomed the food. "There isn't any more, is there?"

Cerise grinned and called something over her shoulder in what sounded like the aliens' language. One of the natives appeared and handed her two more leaves. Another alien—this one clearly female, with a band across her chest—handed them both what looked like upturned turtle shells filled with water.

"Should I drink it?" True asked Cerise as she held her shell with both hands.

"It's water they collect from dew on the leaves," Cerise told her, tipping her own water into her mouth. "It's safe."

"Good to know," True muttered to herself, draining her water shell and then starting in on the flafaya. She glanced down at the ground below. "Should we see if Varden and Kos are hungry?"

"We can't," Cerise said, setting her empty leaves inside the bare shell. "They left early this morning."

True dropped her now-empty leaf, and it fluttered to the floor. "Gone? They left us?"

Cerise giggled as she shook her head. "They went to check on the ship."

"You mean the ship that sank?"

Now the Perogling bobbed her head up and down. "I heard them talking as they left. They're hoping to salvage the part of the ship that can send out a distress call."

"That's good," True said, her mind now filled with worry for the two Drexians. She hoped Varden didn't have the urge to play the hero again, since yesterday it had almost killed him.

"I'm sure they'll be fine. They are Drexians, after all."

"Right." True forced herself to smile. "Of course. I'm not worried."

"Mmhmm." Cerise cocked a perfectly arched brow at her. "I can tell."

"What?" True's face warmed. "Okay, I'm a little worried. I just know how they are, and I'm afraid they're going to get killed being brave badasses."

"They are pretty impressive, especially when they take their clothes off."

"Cerise!"

The little woman leaned back and laughed. "Don't tell me you haven't noticed, because I'll know you're lying. I saw the way you looked at him last night."

True opened her mouth to protest, but closed it. She knew it was pointless to argue. "Fine, but it's not like it matters. Nothing's ever going to happen."

"Why not? I thought things had already happened?"

True shook her head hard. "That's in the past. We agreed to forget about all that and start fresh, as if we'd never met before yesterday."

Cerise stared at her. "Excuse me?"

"You know, a clean slate, a reset, a do-over."

"I do *not* know," Cerise said. "You can't forget having kissed a man like that, and I can tell you right now, he's sure not going to forget it."

Heat coursed through True's body as she flashed back to the feel of his soft lips moving urgently against hers. A throb of desire twitched between her legs, proving Cerise right and her very wrong.

"It doesn't matter." She shifted uncomfortably on the bumpy bound branches. "He's the captain of the Boat. He's experienced in everything. I'd never even kissed a man before him. He deserves someone who knows...well, things."

Cerise waved a hand at her as if she was shooing away a fly. "Don't you worry your pretty little head. I can tell you everything you need to know to drive any male wild."

Her heart hammered in her chest at the thought. "I don't want to drive him wild."

"Sure you do, sweetie. You just don't know it yet."

True shook her head vigorously. "It's not the same as in a pleasure house. I can't do things a..."

Cerise leveled her gaze at her. "A whore would do? Isn't that what you Earthlings call your pleasurers?"

"I didn't mean that," True said. This was going from bad to worse.

Cerise giggled again. "Oh, I don't mind. Being a pleasurer isn't something to be ashamed of on every world." She winked at True. "And I was very good at what I did."

"I'm sure you were, but..." True spun a strand of hair around one finger.

"Listen." Cerise leaned forward. "Do you have feelings for the captain?"

True nodded. She did, even if she couldn't say it out loud.

"If you want him, one day you'll have to do more than kiss him. Not that kissing isn't great—sometimes it's the best part—but I'd hate for that fine Drexian's balls to turn blue and fall off."

True blinked rapidly. "Can that really happen?"

Cerise patted her hand. "No, not really. You really are clueless, aren't you?" She sighed. "Have you ever actually seen a cock?"

"In real life?" True asked, then bit her lower lip. "No."

"Well, I'm not going to lie to you. Drexians have big ones. Huge, actually."

True squeezed her legs together involuntarily. "What if I can't...?"

"Oh, you can. It might take a little patience." Cerise patted her knee. "And it might not be a bad idea to bite down on something at first."

"Really?" She fanned herself. The hot, humid air was not helping things.

"I'm teasing," Cerise said, then tilted her head to one side. "Maybe just bite on him the first time. He'll like that, anyway."

"He will?" True couldn't imagine enjoying being bitten, but the idea of biting one of his smooth, hard muscles gave her a little thrill. "What else would he like?"

Cerise scooted closer. "I can't speak for all males, but the ones I've sampled love it when a female lets them know she's having a good time."

"How do I do that?"

Cerise dabbed some moisture off her upper lip. "Some of it you won't be able to help—moaning, screaming, panting—but if you want to drive them over the edge, you need to talk."

True pulled Varden's shirt away from her sticky skin, moving it quickly to get some air. "Talk? About what?"

"Not *about* anything, silly. Talk dirty."

True straightened up. She couldn't ever imagine saying anything dirty to someone like Varden. Despite what he'd said to her, which she knew was a slip he'd regretted. He was so, well, distinguished. "I don't think he'd like that."

"Trust me, honey. They all like it. Even the silver foxes who command entire space stations like a girl to tell them how huge their cock is."

"You want me to say that?" True's voice cracked. "About his...cock?"

Cerise slapped her leg. "See? That wasn't so hard, was it?"

Actually, True thought she very well might pass out and roll off the platform onto the ground.

"Now, try this," Cerise said, pitching her voice higher. "I love riding your big cock."

True swallowed hard. "I love riding your big...cock."

"A little stiff, but it's a start. At least you didn't blush when you said cock." Cerise glanced at True's hot cheeks. "Well, any more than you already are, I mean."

"What else should I say?" True asked, feeling empowered now that she could say cock without fainting.

Cerise drummed her stubby fingers on her chin. "Tell him how much he's stretching you, which he will be. Tell him he's splitting you in two."

True let out a small squeak.

"Not literally," Cerise said, quickly. "Not even a Drexian can split you into two pieces. Now a Xakden on the other hand..." She shivered. "Let's get back to the fun stuff. Males love it when you beg them."

True wrinkled her nose. "Beg them?"

"Beg them," Cerise said. "Tell him you want him to fuck you. That word coming from someone like you might send him over the edge."

True wasn't sure she'd ever be able to tell a man that. Even thinking the word made her flinch. "How about I just talk about his cock some more?"

Cerise shrugged. "Okay, let me hear what you've got."

True took a deep breath, reminding herself that nobody within earshot—except for Cerise—could understand a word she was saying. She tried to make her voice breathy and girly at the same time. "Oooo, that's a big one!"

Cerise clapped. "Excellent, and very believable."

Alien chatter made the Perogling look up, her face breaking into an even wider smile. "Varden and Kos are back!"

FIFTEEN

Kos stopped short as they reached the village, and Varden almost ran into him.

They were both soaked to the bone after barely pulling themselves up through the hatches before the ship filled completely with water. They'd swum to the side of the pond and dragged themselves out, then watched as the ship disappeared under the surface. Again.

The dripping Drexians had walked back through the jungle in near silence, following the trail of luminescent marks on the tree trunks and leaves. What was there to say? The ship was truly a loss now, and there would be no beacon to alert the Drexians to their location. They had to hope that someone had intercepted that original transmission, although the longer they went without a rescue, the greater the chance that no one had.

Just as Varden was about to wonder how much longer they needed to walk, he heard True's breathy voice from above him.

"Oooo, that's a big one."

Kos jerked to a stop, and Varden had to grab his arms to keep from running headlong into him. A few of the natives called down to them, but Varden could only make out that it was a greeting of some kind. Both men stared up into the trees without saying a word, and a moment later, Cerise's head popped over the edge of the platform.

"They were right. You're back!"

Varden cleared his throat. "Is everything all right up there?"

"Oh, yes. Just a little girl talk."

Kos choked on what Varden thought must have been a stifled laugh and mumbled something about drying his pants before climbing up a different ladder.

Varden remained standing in the clearing underneath the vertical village, not knowing quite what to do. He'd never heard True sound like that—not even when they'd been on the holodeck—and her teasing voice made his cock throb. What did it mean when Cerise had said "girl talk"? What kind of girl talk made True sound breathless and sexy? And what was "a big one"?

The more he thought about what she'd said, the harder he got, until he felt like he might explode. He staggered away, hurriedly pulling the luminescence from his pack and marking the trees as he went. After he'd gotten far enough away from the village, and True, he leaned against a tree trunk and steadied his breath.

He had to get himself together. They were supposed to forget about anything that had happened between them, but a few words from her and he was right back on the holodeck, feeling her arch against him as her tongue tangled with his. He didn't know what he was going to do if they weren't rescued soon. No way would he survive living in such close proximity to a woman he craved so completely.

His cock still ached, straining against his soaked pants, but as he concentrated on breathing in and out, he heard something that piqued his interest. Flowing water, and lots of it.

He pushed his way through the jungle and toward the noise, staring when he reached a gap in the trees. Across the opening, a waterfall at least two metrons high poured down from a high rock ledge, the blue water pooling below and trailing off into a stream that twisted deeper into the jungle. Steam rose from the water as it cascaded down, and some of the spray formed a fine mist that hit his face.

He blinked hard a few times to make sure he wasn't imagining it. It was possible that the stress from the past two days had made him delusional. Or maybe his horrific case of blue balls was the cause, although he'd never heard of hallucinations as a side effect. He touched the warm mist on his face. But he wouldn't be able to *feel* a hallucination, would he?

Kicking off his shoes, Varden walked to the edge of the water, dipping one toe in gingerly. He almost groaned with pleasure. The water was blissfully warm, even warmer than the thermal springs on Candor Prime. He tugged off his pants and peeled his underwear from his body, leaving his clothes in a pile on the ground as he lowered himself into the pool. When his toes touched the bottom, he was pleased to feel rock instead of mud, and he bent his knees until he was submerged up to his neck.

He could feel the tension in his body begin to disappear as the steaming water did its work. Maybe this wasn't a bad place to be stranded, after all. He backed up until the waterfall was pounding against his shoulders, keeping his eyes closed as spray shot out in all directions. When his back began to sting, he moved away, sinking down below the surface again.

As good as the hot water felt, it hadn't done anything about his hard cock. Actually, the heat made it throb even more. Varden stood so that the water reached his waist. He reached under the water and fisted his cock, keeping his eyes closed as he listened to the rushing water behind him.

He let his mind wander as he slowly dragged his hand up and down his shaft. He could hear her high voice in his head, and he imagined she was talking about him, that it was his cock making her breathless.

Groaning, he pumped harder as he thought about how she'd felt when she'd straddled him on the holodeck. The feel of her soft skin underneath his hands, the way she'd moved on him. He'd been hard then, too, and the sensation of her rubbing against his cock had made him want to flip her on her back and plunge himself into her.

He knew her tight heat would feel incredible stretching around him, and he moaned as he envisioned her beneath him. A sound that was not the rushing of water made him freeze, and his eyes flew open.

True stood on the edge of the pool in his oversized uniform shirt, and only the back of Cerise's bobbing wig was visible as she slipped back into the jungle. Her eyes were wide as she stared at him, her gaze moving down his body and locking on to what was beneath the water.

Releasing his grip on his cock, he dipped down so that his entire body was underwater. "I'm sorry. You weren't supposed to see that."

Her tongue licked her lower lip, and then she bit one corner. "It's okay." Her eyes met his. "I liked it."

Well, that didn't help. His cock rose up almost instantly, and he had to use both hands to cover it. "I thought you wanted to forget everything between us."

She hitched in a breath. "I think I changed my mind." She glanced down again. "About all of it."

He almost came on the spot, squeezing his eyes together and willing himself to think about anything except what sweet, innocent True had just said to him. He bit back a groan. "True—" he began, but then he opened his eyes and saw that she was slowly unbuttoning her shirt—correction, his shirt.

He tried to swallow, but his mouth was dry as he watched her slip off the oversized military shirt and stand on the edge of the water in her pale pink bra and panties. Her face was flushed and her pupils wide, making her blue eyes look darker than usual.

She eased herself into the water and made her way over to him.

Standing up, he dropped his hands, and his cock jutted out from his body. She stopped and pressed shaking fingers to his taut stomach. "I think this is the part where I tell you I want you."

CHAPTER
SIXTEEN

She didn't know what had gotten into her. Maybe it was because they were stuck on an alien planet with no sign of rescue, or maybe it was the heat making her all hot and bothered, but whatever the reason, True felt bolder than she ever had.

Not that she wasn't still scared. She was, and as she reached out to touch him, her hand trembled visibly. When she pressed it against his warm skin, the corded muscles hard beneath her fingers, he covered it with his own.

"Are you sure?" His words were muffled by the sound of the waterfall, but she thought she heard his voice crack.

Was she sure? She looked up at his face, his crystal-blue eyes flashing desire as his breath heaved in his chest. He stood completely still—every muscle in his body seemed to be coiled like a spring—as he held his hand gently over hers.

She gulped. He was still massive, but as she stood in front of his naked body, she found his size comforting instead of terrifying. He would never let anything bad happen to her, and he would never hurt her. She knew that without a doubt. Even now, he held himself back, refusing to do anything until she promised him that she was sure.

She'd let her fears—and the stories she'd been told growing up—hold her back for so long, and it hadn't done her a bit of good except to leave her isolated. Her two closest friends on the Boat had found love and gone to live with their Drexians, while she'd avoided contact with any male on the station. Except the one she'd thought wasn't real.

She didn't even care about that anymore. She'd been more embarrassed than angry, anyway, but now none of that mattered. All that mattered was that he was the same person she'd fallen for on the holodeck, the same person she dreamed about, the same person who made her think things she'd never thought before. Hell, yeah, she was sure.

True took a small step forward and nodded. "I want this. I want you."

As if she'd unleashed him from invisible chains, Varden crushed his mouth to hers, wrapping his arms around her and lifting her feet from the rock floor. She tried to breathe as his mouth plundered hers, his tongue parting her lips, but he rendered her breathless.

He moved his hands down to cup her ass, then hoisted her so she was straddling him, her legs wound tightly around his waist. She rocked her hips into him, feeling an ache of need between her legs and then hot surges of pleasure as the silk of her panties rubbed his ridged stomach.

One of his hands slid up to tangle in her hair, pulling her deeper into the kiss. She gripped his slick shoulders, her fingers biting into his muscles and then slipping down his back to brush against his nodes.

Varden let out a desperate growl, jerking her body in tighter.

True was no longer submerged in the steaming water, but liquid heat fired her belly and made her heart race. Her pulse skittered wildly as she felt herself bump against his cock.

Varden pulled back, and his molten eyes locked with hers. "Tell me what you like."

She dropped her gaze, focusing on the pulsing vein in his neck. "I don't know. I've never..."

His body stiffened. "Never? You're a...?"

She nodded, afraid to look up and see the disappointment in his eyes. Of course he wouldn't want a virgin, someone who didn't know what she was doing. "I'm sorry. It's okay if you don't want to—"

He swallowed her words with a deep kiss, his tongue stroking her until she'd sunk boneless into him with a husky moan.

"My sweet, perfect True," he murmured when they finally parted. "How could you ever think I wouldn't want you?"

He kissed his way down her neck, lifting her higher so he could suck her nipples through the thin, wet fabric of her bra. Dropping her head back, she cried out as he nipped her gently, lavishing attention on first one breast and then the other until she was writhing beneath his hot mouth. Her hands roamed his back, brushing his hard nodes and feeling the pulsing heat as his arousal grew. She loved the dark rumble in his throat that grew louder the faster she stroked.

Varden's grip on her ass tightened, his fingers so close to her opening she knew he could feel her wetness.

"Please," she gasped, arching into him, needing more.

He slid her back down until she bumped up against his rigid length. She sucked in a breath when she felt it, startled once again by its size and by how desperately she wanted to ride it.

She took his face in her hands and met his hungry gaze. "I need you inside me."

He closed his eyes for a moment, as if to steady himself, then opened them and cupped her face in his hand. "I don't want to hurt you."

Her heart was pounding so hard, she was afraid she might die if she didn't get some release. Turning her head to capture one of his fingers in her mouth, she sucked on it hard.

"*Grek,* True." His words were choked. "You're sure you've never done this before?" He lowered them both down into the water, kissing her softly as he did. "The heat will help stretch you so you can take me."

Butterflies fluttered in her stomach as he moved aside her panties, his fingers teasing her opening. "Do you want my fingers first?"

She shook her head, her hands clutching his shoulders, remembering what Cerise had taught her. "I want your big cock."

He bit down on his lower lip, groaning. "This does not help me take you slow."

"Sorry." Her breath was ragged as she felt his thick crown nudge her opening.

His lips brushed hers softly, then his tongue opened her mouth and heat rolled through her as he kissed her deeply, his hands clutching the sides of her hips and guiding her down. She could feel herself stretching as he pushed his cock slowly inside, the burning sensation making her inhale sharply. Before she could tell him she might have changed her mind, he gave a hard thrust and was inside her completely.

True's screams were swallowed by his kiss, and he held himself deep as she tried to catch her breath. She struggled to get away, but his grip on her hips was firm, and soon the discomfort went away.

"Are you okay?" he asked, his voice strained when he finally tore his mouth from hers.

"Mmhmm." She leaned her forehead against his, feeling his warm breath on her cheek. "Are you?"

He gave a hoarse laugh. "Never been better." He stroked a finger down her cheek. "I didn't hurt you too much?"

True rocked her hips forward, making him let out a strangled breath, as she savored the feeling of being filled by him completely.

So this was what everyone was talking about. Now she got it. Even as the memory of the initial sting lingered, she relished the feel of his big cock inside her, their bodies locked together.

She nipped one of his earlobes, then whispered, "You can hurt me like this as much as you want."

SEVENTEEN

H er words were like rocket fuel, shooting through his body and igniting his desire. He pulled out and thrust himself in again, hearing her breathy gasp.

"This is what you want?" Varden asked, watching her throw her head back.

She nodded, her lips pressed together, her cheeks flushed.

He clenched his jaw as he moved her up and down on his shaft, her heat stretching for him. "So tight, True. You're so wet and so tight for me."

He'd never felt so complete before. Being inside this pretty human felt more right than anything he could imagine. He took in her pale hair tousled around her face and her teeth biting on her lower lip. "Look at me, True."

Her eyes opened and focused on him. He felt like he could get lost in her wide blue eyes, and he cradled the back of her head with one hand, holding her face only inches from his.

The desire to claim True as his mate slammed into him. He needed her to be his and only his, and the craving to have her threatened to level him.

"You are mine," he said, stroking into her. "Only mine."

She let out a soft noise, her eyes fluttering. "Yes, Varden."

"Tell me," he said, panting as he stroked deep. "Tell me you are mine."

"I'm yours," she said, her eyes flaring.

Water splashed around them as he worked her up and down. "Do you like this? Me claiming you with my cock?"

A husky cry escaped her lips as he plunged into her and held himself deep. "I love you fucking me."

Gods, the woman drove him insane. He loved hearing dirty words spilling out of her sweet little mouth.

Teeth clenched, he impaled her on his length again and again, their screams mingling and drowning out the sounds of the pounding waterfall and the rushing of blood inside his own head. He tilted her hips forward to rub against her swollen nub, feeling her jerk as his own release built.

Varden held back, fighting the urge to explode as he rocked his body slowly so that it teased her bundle of nerves. She thrashed, her eyes rolling back in her head. "Please, Varden."

He felt a rush as he watched her writhe. She was his. Her pleasure, her passion, her gasps of desire. All his. "Please what, cinnara?"

"I don't know," she said, her fingernails digging into his back. "Just more, harder, *please*."

Her urgent tone made his body detonate, and he crushed his mouth to hers, kissing her with a furious need as he pulsed hot into her. She made high-pitched keening noises, clamping around his cock as she came, her nails scoring his shoulders.

After a moment, they both sank lower into the water, breathing heavily and quivering. He pulled her closer, wrapping his arms around her and tucking her head beneath his chin as he stroked her hair. He knew he should regret what he'd said to her, how much he'd needed her to accept his claim on her body, but he didn't. He felt nothing but connection as her heartbeat echoed through his own chest.

"Is it always like that?" True asked in a quiet voice.

"No." He pulled back and traced a finger along her jaw. "You were incredible."

Her cheeks were a patchwork of pink and red, but she smiled shyly up at him. "I didn't know it could be like *that*."

He chuckled. "You are sure I didn't hurt you?"

She shrugged. "I don't think I can walk anymore, but it was worth it."

"I am happy to carry you around for the rest of our lives."

Her cheeks flushed deeper. "I know it's supposed to be wrong, but it didn't feel wrong. It actually felt really right."

He dragged his thumb across her plump lower lip. "Why would this be wrong?"

Her eyes dropped. "When I grew up, I was told that sex was a sin unless it was between married people. And even then, it wasn't supposed to be for fun. Only to make babies. You weren't supposed to like it, especially women. Only loose women actually liked it."

Varden stared at her. No wonder she'd been a virgin until now. "Loose?"

"You know, a woman who gets around, who has sex with a lot of men."

"A pleasurer? Well, you are hardly one of those, yet you enjoyed it, did you not?"

She swatted at his chest. "You know I did."

"Then what they told you can't be correct." He lifted her chin with one finger. "I do not believe what we did was bad; do you?"

She twitched one shoulder up. "If it was, I think I'm fine with that, because I definitely want to do it again."

"Now?" His cock was still inside her and still hard, but he hadn't wanted to make her even more sore than she already was.

She laughed. "Maybe not right now. I think I need a bit of a rest."

He released her legs and let them drop to the stone bottom of the pool. "Can you stand?"

"Of course I can stand—" she began, before her legs went wobbly. He caught her by the arm to keep her from falling.

"Okay, maybe I need a second." She slipped a hand into his, squeezing it as she glanced around them. "I like this pool. Amazing something like this is out here in the middle of the jungle. How did you find it?"

"By accident," he said. "How did you find me?"

"Cerise had one of the natives track you after you stormed out of the village."

His face warmed. "I needed to blow off some frustration."

"Frustration with me?" she asked.

He brushed a strand of hair out of her face. "Not *with* you. It's been difficult being so close to you and not being able to..."

"I know. It's been hard for me, too. I've wanted to jump you from the moment you ran onto the holodeck."

He still couldn't believe the human wanted him over any other Drexian. She was so young and beautiful. He decided not to think about how he didn't deserve her, and just enjoy the moment. "You trust me?"

She met his gaze, moving her head up and down. "Completely."

His chest swelled, and he kissed her softly. "Close your eyes."

She grinned and closed them, holding on to his shoulders as he backed her up until the water from the falls was hitting her back, sending spray ricocheting through the air. She squealed in delight, keeping her eyes closed and laughing when Varden finally rotated so they were both under the flowing water. After a moment, he took another step back, and they were behind the rushing water.

There was a pocket of about half a metron between them and the rock wall—enough to stand without getting drenched. The sound of the waterfall drowned out all other noise, but he didn't need to hear her to know how happy she was.

She raked her fingers through his hair, drawing him into her for a deep kiss. She moved her lips to hover beside his ear, her furtive words sending a hum of pleasure shooting down his spine and warming his nodes almost instantly. "I think I'm ready for you to fuck me again."

CHAPTER
EIGHTEEN

True felt a tingle between her legs and let out a sigh. His fingers skimmed along her inner thigh, his touch so tender, she shivered. Letting her legs fall open for him, she bit back a moan, then rolled over and off the mat.

She flinched as she jerked awake, blinking rapidly as the walled platform came into focus, as well as the trees surrounding it. She'd been dreaming about him again. She didn't have to touch her panties to know they were damp. Again.

Since the waterfall, she'd been dreaming about Varden every night, often waking several times flushed with sweat, her nipples hard and her thighs slick. She'd gone from virgin to sex-crazed, she thought, shaking her head and pushing her hair out of her face.

It wasn't like she had anything to complain about. He'd taken her back to the waterfall several times in the past two days, and each time had been amazing. He still felt huge when he entered her, but the discomfort had vanished, and now it was nothing but delicious pleasure. Her body heated in response to her wandering thoughts, and she let out an impatient breath.

Even though Varden made no secret of how he felt about her when they were alone, he hadn't wanted to share their relationship with the others. He'd said it was best if they kept things between them private, and she'd agreed. But that meant sleeping alone and resisting the urge to touch him when they were around Kos or Cerise or even the natives, although she doubted any of them were clueless about what had gone on. The waterfall wasn't that far away, and they weren't very quiet.

"Good morning," Cerise said, dropping down onto the platform from above. "I wondered when you'd ever wake up."

True stretched. "Is it very late?"

Cerise shrugged. "Later than usual." She eyed her. "Did you sleep at all?"

No way was True going to tell the Perogling that she was tired because she'd had sex dreams all night long. She motioned to the mat. "It's not exactly the most comfortable thing to sleep on."

"You should try one of the hammocks. They're like sleeping on air."

"That's because they're hanging in midair." True cut her eyes to where hammocks were strung up high between trees. "If I rolled over, I'd drop fifty feet. I'll stick with the hard mat, thanks."

"Suit yourself." Cerise settled herself cross-legged and handed True a leaf filled with fruit. "I ate ages ago, but I saved some for you."

True smiled, shaking off her exhaustion. "That was sweet of you. Thanks." She took a bite, savoring the kick of heat. "Has everyone else already eaten?"

"If by everyone you mean the sexy captain you're boning, then yes. He and Kos ate earlier before heading out."

True started to protest that they weren't boning, but she realized that Cerise would never be fooled by her lies. That, and she got caught up on the last part of what the alien had said. "Headed out? Where did they go?"

"They wanted to find the highest spot in the jungle and see if they could set up some sort of signal with their one communication device." Cerise leaned closer, her wig almost touching True's forehead. "If you ask me, it's a waste of time, but you know males. They have to be doing something or they feel useless."

True swallowed. She had to agree with her friend. The chances of getting any sort of signal off the planet with one puny communication device was pretty slim, but she also knew that the Drexians were getting antsy after being stuck on the planet for several days now. As friendly and hospitable as the natives were, she knew neither Drexian welcomed the thought of living on the jungle planet permanently.

The idea didn't drive her wild, either. She was still wearing Varden's uniform shirt, although now it was dingy and rumpled, and she craved a real bed and a cup of coffee. She'd even be grateful for some of the Drexian coffee substitute.

She also missed her friends, the other independent women from the Boat and the tribute brides she'd gotten to know. By now, everyone had probably gathered at the rendezvous point. She wondered if they'd sent out a search party like Varden was convinced they would have, and if they had any clues to go on or if they were wandering aimlessly through the galaxy searching for a homing beacon or distress call.

She finished her fruit and wiped her mouth with the leaf as Cerise gave her a Cheshire-cat grin. "What? Do I have something on my face?"

"No, nothing like that. I just wonder when you're going to admit that you're in love with him."

True stared at the woman's arched brow. "In love?"

"I know you're banging him. I mean, I could hear it from here, sweetie. But I also know you aren't the type to do that unless you're all in. So, are you?"

True's face heated under the alien's scrutiny. "Am I what?"

"All in? In love? Head over heels?" Cerise leaned back, tilting her head. "Or are you just obsessed with his cock?"

Now True's face really burned. "I'm not just obsessed with his cock!"

"That's what I thought. Not that I'm sure it isn't spectacular. I can tell just by looking at him that it would be." She winked at True. "It's one of my special talents, being able to look at a man and tell you what type of cock he has. And let me tell you, that's come in handy quite a lot over the years."

True waved her hands to stop the torrent of words. "Okay, I give. You win. I did it. I mean, we did it. I slept with him."

"If you ask me, there wasn't much sleeping going on, but I know you humans like to use that particular phrase." She patted True's leg. "How was it? Did you take my advice?"

"Some of it," True said, shifting uncomfortably as she remembered talking dirty to Varden. "It was good. Really good. Better than I imagined."

Cerise clapped her hands. "I'm so happy. Not that I expected it to be anything less than spectacular. Just look at him." She fanned herself with both hands. "I get all hot and bothered thinking about him prancing around here without a shirt."

True couldn't help giggling. Varden would die if he heard Cerise talking about him like that. "He doesn't prance, and the only reason he's shirtless is because I have no clothes, and it's a thousand degrees."

"That's true." Cerise dabbed her moist upper lip, then glanced at the mat on the floor. "So if you two are together, why are you still sleeping alone?"

Good question, thought True. "I don't think the captain is the type to let everyone into his personal life. He said he wanted to keep things private."

"Sweetie. We're in the middle of a jungle. There are no walls anywhere. Trust me when I tell you that what you two are doing is not private."

True swallowed hard, pushing her mother's warning about wanton women from her mind. "I know, but that's different than sharing a bed together. If we did that, it would mean..."

What would it mean, she wondered? That what they were doing

was more than sex? That it wasn't just them both scratching itches that had desperately needed scratching? That she was his mate?

True didn't know what Varden thought about taking a mate. Clearly, he'd never taken a tribute bride, and she could only assume he'd had plenty of chances. If he'd wanted one, couldn't the captain of the Boat have simply requested one? Maybe he had no intention of taking a mate. Maybe all of this was just fun for him.

No. She shook her head. He wouldn't use her like that. She knew he wouldn't.

"What would it mean?" Cerise asked, her brows pressed together.

"It might weaken his authority with his first officer," she finally said. "Kos looks up to him. I doubt he wants to cross that line with someone who serves under him."

Cerise tapped her chin, as if considering this. "That makes sense, although I'm not sure it matters about command structure and rank anymore. Especially if we're stuck here for the long haul."

She had a point. Would he still be considered the captain if they had to live on the planet long term? Her stomach tightened. Part of her was desperate to get rescued, and another part of her knew that would be the end of whatever was going on between them. It was like the holodeck all over again, she thought, and she wasn't sure if she could give up the fantasy of him again.

CHAPTER
NINETEEN

Varden stopped to catch his breath as they crested the hill. The native leading them chattered something in his language, his face breaking into a wide smile. The jungle had parted as they'd walked higher, and the peak of what could generously be called a hill was bare of trees.

Varden's auditory translator managed to decipher enough of the words so that he knew the alien was telling him this was the highest point. He sighed. It wasn't much of a summit, although he hadn't been expecting a mountain. From what he'd learned about the planet, it was all flat terrain covered by dense jungle.

"This is it?" Kos asked, not hiding his disappointment.

"It's better than nothing," he told his first officer, although he agreed with the young Drexian.

As it was, their attempt to get a transmission off using his comms device was a long shot. He'd hoped a higher point would give their signal a greater chance, but he doubted this would make much of a difference. If he was being honest with himself, he was beginning to lose hope of being rescued.

He knew it had only been a few days, but the fact that no ships had entered the atmosphere told him that their initial transmission had not been received. Whatever search party was out there looking for them—and he knew there was one—was flying blind. No one had any clue what route they'd taken or where they'd crashed. It could take weeks or months to search every possible route and all possible planets along the way.

"I'll get started," Kos said, taking the comms device they'd altered and setting it up on the ground.

Varden rocked back on his heels as he watched his officer work. Would it be so bad if the rescue was delayed? It wasn't that he wanted to stay on this primitive planet forever, but he couldn't deny how much he was enjoying his waterfall interludes with True. He pressed down on his cock as it strained against his pants, glad that his fellow Drexian was so absorbed in his work and that the green-skinned alien was looking off in another direction.

No matter how many times they snuck away, he couldn't get enough of her—the feel of her tight heat, the taste of her soft skin, the sound of her soft gasps as he drove his cock into her. She was everything he'd ever wanted in a female. Everything he could ever imagine wanting in a mate.

He hesitated, reminding himself that he shouldn't think of her as his mate. She was an independent, and as far as he knew, she had never had any intention of taking a Drexian mate. It was why she'd liked the idea of a holographic man, and why he knew he couldn't get his hopes up. As crazy as he was about her, and as much as he couldn't imagine being without her, he had to be realistic. She was a beautiful young Earthling who could have any Drexian she wanted. Or none at all.

The idea of True with another Drexian made him curl his hands into fists. He couldn't bear the thought of her with anyone but him, realistic or not. She was his. She had been since he'd first laid eyes on her in her holodeck simulation.

His gaze fell on Kos as he worked to set up their makeshift beacon. Did he really want to be rescued and risk everything with

True? The thought of sabotaging their attempt flitted through his mind, then back out again.

Grek. What was wrong with him? Was his obsession with True addling his brain? He couldn't live the rest of his life in this primitive jungle. Neither could she. And he certainly couldn't sentence Kos to that fate.

As it was, he hadn't mentioned anything about True to his first mate. He suspected the warrior knew, but he also knew his officer would never mention it. Despite the situation, he was still the captain, and Kos was a member of his crew. Granted, his most loyal and devoted member.

He glanced at the dark-haired Drexian working diligently on the ground. At times like this, Varden wished he was anything *but* the commanding officer of the Boat. He wished he could just be one of the guys again, joking about battles and females like he had when he was a young warrior. But he wasn't that Drexian anymore, and he needed to keep the command structure in place, even if they were stranded on an alien planet. Perhaps, *especially* if they were stranded on an alien planet.

He and True had agreed to keep their relationship private, but he hated feeling like it was something to hide. He wanted nothing more than to tell the world that she was his, but he also didn't want the questions and looks that would invariably come when people saw her with him. How would he explain to Drexian High Command that he'd claimed a human female when warriors half his age were waiting for years? He doubted it would go over well.

"It's transmitting, sir," Kos said as he stood. "But I don't know how much reach it has."

Neither warrior said what they were undoubtedly thinking. The only way a ship would pick up on a signal this weak was if they were hovering above the surface.

"Good work." Varden clapped a hand on Kos's shoulder.

The first officer shrugged. "Like you said, it's better than nothing."

The alien with the long black braid had leapt up to a tree edging the clearing, and his chattering made them both look over at him. He perched on a branch, his dark-rimmed eyes narrowed on the horizon.

"Did he say something about a bird?" Kos asked.

Varden concentrated on the jumbled half-words being processed by his universal translator. "A black bird."

Both men glanced around. They hadn't seen black birds in this jungle. Every creature here appeared to be brightly colored, and many of them were phosphorescent.

"I don't think our translators know how to cope with their language," Kos said with a snort. "Unless this guy can see something we can't."

Before Kos could respond, a dark space ship appeared in the distance. His heart leapt. The Drexians had heard their transmission. A rescue had finally arrived. As he turned to celebrate with Kos, his eyes caught a detail on the approaching ship. He squinted as it approached, his stomach hardening into a pit. The gunmetal-gray hull wasn't smooth like on Drexian ships. It was covered in a scale-like armor.

"Kronock." Kos said the word like a curse.

Varden grabbed his arm and pulled him out of sight as the fighter flew low, the wings skimming the trees. The roar of the engine was deafening, and he could feel the heat from the exhaust burn his neck as he bent low.

When the ship had passed, he located the native still high in the tree, clutching the swaying branch, his face stricken. The alien emitted more chatter and pointed wildly toward the jungle as the ship stopped and hovered.

"Home," Kos said, repeating the one word they'd both understood.

Fear slammed into Varden as he realized what the alien meant. The treetop village. The Kronock were targeting the alien village.

"True," he whispered as he took off running.

TWENTY

"Hold it from the base," Cerise said, clutching the hard cylindrical pod in one hand as True watched. "Move that hand up and down while you take your mouth—"

"Did you hear that?" True asked, interrupting her friend's lesson and dropping her own pod onto the platform, the dried seeds spilling across the bound tree trunks.

The usual buzz of alien chatter and the cawing of birds overhead had been replaced by a low hum, but it wasn't a natural noise. It sounded like an engine.

Cerise cocked her head to one side. "That's odd."

True stood, holding on to the edge of the short wall and poking her head out from underneath the thatched roof. She peered up, shielding her eyes from the two glowing suns, whose rays peeked through the canopy of leaves. "I think it's a ship."

Cerise's bright coral mouth formed a perfect O of surprise. "The Drexians found us? We're rescued?"

True's stomach did a somersault, and she wasn't sure if it was from excitement or anxiety. On the one hand, she really wanted to get back to civilization, but on the other, she was afraid that leaving the planet would break the magic between her and Varden. What if they were having a "shipboard romance" that would dissolve into thin air once they returned to reality?

"Can you see them yet?" Cerise asked, joining her at the edge of the platform and looking up.

The sound got louder, and True saw the alien natives hopping from tree to tree, apparently evacuating the village. She wanted to yell to them that it was all right, that these were their friends. But she knew no one could hear her over the roaring, and they couldn't understand her language even if they could make out her words.

Cerise's hand shot out and clamped around her wrist at the same time the ship came into view, hovering above them and blocking out all light. Instead of being sleek and black, like many of the Drexian ships, with a smooth, curved hull, this ship was a muddy gray, with scaly armor.

True's throat constricted. This wasn't a Drexian ship.

She glanced down at her friend, who was tugging on her arm.

Kronock, Cerise mouthed, her eyes filled with terror.

True didn't know many specifics about the alien race that the Drexians considered their sworn enemies. She did know that they were violent, merciless, and bent on the destruction of the Drexians by way of destroying Earth and the Drexians' hope for continuing their species. She also knew from Bridget—a tribute bride who'd been taken by the Kronock—that they were huge, covered in scales, and had augmented themselves with bionic hardware. She'd hoped to never have the occasion to confirm the woman's description.

Cerise tugged at her arm again, this time screaming up at her, "We have to get out of here!"

True's legs were like lead, but she managed to nod in agreement and follow the Perogling down the ladder even though her hands were shaking and her feet slipped on a couple of the rungs. The natives were blurs as they swung through the air above her, their chattering now cries of warning as green searchlights from the ship scanned the trees.

The native True recognized as one of the leaders leapt down in front of them, firing off something in rapid-fire alien-speak and beckoning for them to follow.

"Come on," Cerise yelled. "We need to follow him to safety."

True didn't hesitate. Any place was better than being directly underneath a Kronock ship, the heat of its exhaust wilting leaves around her and blasting her hair out of her face.

She wondered where Varden was and hoped he was safe as they hurried through the jungle. The small alien weaved through the dense foliage effortlessly, his long braid swinging down his back, and cast the occasional look back at them. Cerise stayed close on his heels, moving fast for one so small, and True had to run to keep up with them, lifting her knees high to prevent herself from tripping over knotty roots.

Behind her, she could hear the ship moving, and she wondered if it was scanning every bit of the forest. She could only assume the Kronock were searching for them, and she wondered how the enemy had locked on to their location before the Drexians. No way the makeshift beacon Varden and Kos had gone to set up had worked so quickly, if at all.

After a few minutes, True's breath was ragged, and sweat ran in rivulets down her back. A steamy jungle was not the place to do cardio, she told herself, wiping the sweat from her brow before it dripped into her eyes.

Just as she was about to ask for a break, she heard a different sound—rushing water. They'd reached her waterfall! The alien pushed through a last curtain of vines, and True saw the crystal-blue water cascading over the high rocks. Her thoughts returned immediately to Varden and memories of all the delicious things they'd done in the warm waters.

The alien jabbed a finger toward the falls. She knew exactly what he wanted them to do.

"He wants us to hide in the waterfall," she told Cerise, already lowering herself into the pool and feeling the steamy water envelop her lower body.

Cerise shook her head. "It will crush us."

True shook her head. "There's space behind it. We just can't tell from here. That means the Kronock will never think to look for us there."

Cerise had gone pale beneath her faded tire-track blush. "I can't swim."

What was it with all these aliens who couldn't swim? True knew that another tribute bride's mate had been unable to swim, and she'd almost drowned him—accidentally, of course.

True stole a quick glance overhead and spotted the edge of the Kronock ship moving in their direction. She waved her hand urgently at Cerise. "Come on. I'll hold you up."

Cerise hesitated, and the native said something to her in his chirpy language.

"Would you rather be captured by the Kronock?" True asked.

That did it. Cerise jumped into the water, drenching the already-damp Drexian military shirt True wore. Grabbing her friend under the arms, True walked backward toward the rushing water, watching as the small native dashed back into the jungle.

"Hold your breath," she cried out moments before taking them both under the pounding torrent of water and emerging on the other side. The pocket of air behind the water was dim, with light diffracted through the wall of rushing water. Despite the noise, the place felt serene to True, and she released a long breath.

Cerise spluttered and coughed, wiping the water out of her eyes. Bright streaks of makeup ran down her pale blue cheeks, making it look like a pair of rainbows extending from underneath her eyes.

True set the woman down, since the water didn't rise above her chest, and leaned against the cool rock wall. She gave her friend the "okay" hand signal with a questioning look. Cerise looked affronted and put both hands on her hips.

True glanced down at her hand and laughed. "I'm asking if you're okay," she shouted over the steady roar of the water.

Realization dawned on Cerise's face, and she grinned. "That's not what that means in a pleasure house."

True laughed again, but she didn't blush. Since losing her virginity to Varden and realizing how much she actually liked sex, she wasn't as easily embarrassed as she used to be. Her best friend Ella would be surprised when she saw her again.

If she saw her again, True reminded herself. She was still marooned on an alien planet with no way off, and now the Kronock were looking for them. At least she and Cerise were safe. As long as the Kronock didn't think to look behind the waterfall.

That was more than she could say for Varden and Kos. She had no idea where they were, if they'd seen the alien ship in time to hide, or if they'd gone back to the alien village and been captured. Her stomach churned as she considered the possibilities.

They were smart, she told herself. Drexian warriors. They would know not to engage an enemy ship on their own, right? Worry gnawed at her as they waited, and when she realized she was shaking, True lowered herself into the steaming water, letting it reach all the way to her chin.

"I'm sure they're fine," Cerise said loudly, her eyes even with True's as she also bobbed in the water. "They're most likely hiding, as well."

True nodded, but she feared that Varden wouldn't hide. Not if he thought she was in danger. She knew enough about his Drexian protectiveness to know that he would risk his own life if he thought she was in danger. She only hoped that didn't mean doing something stupid. She was going to be really pissed off if he got captured and she and Cerise were stuck by themselves on the planet.

"Don't even think about it, buddy," she murmured to herself. "I have no intention of being queen of the little green aliens."

The water splashed up into her face, and she stood. Something had disturbed the pool—something large enough to make the water level rise. She clutched Cerise and backed them both up as far as they could go, putting a finger over her lips to signal her friend to stay quiet. She hoped a finger on the lips wasn't some kinky alien bordello signal, but luckily Cerise got the idea and went completely still next to her.

True wished she had some sort of weapon. She felt helpless as they stood there waiting for whatever it was to burst through the water, her heart knocking against her ribs so loudly she felt sure it could be heard over the water. Cerise slipped her small hand into True's and squeezed.

Glancing down at the small alien with the rainbow cheeks, she gave her what she hoped was a reassuring smile and squeezed back, even though she was pretty sure she was either going to pass out or throw up. Hulking shadows appeared on the other side of the waterfall, making the light around them even dimmer.

True squared her shoulders, and Cerise slapped a hand over her own mouth, presumably to keep from screaming. If the Kronock had found them, she only hoped they hadn't gotten Varden and Kos. The two Drexians would be their only hope of rescue.

As the creatures stepped through the pounding water, spray went into True's face, and she had to close her eyes, blinking rapidly when she opened them and gaping up at the aliens in front of her. She heard Cerise squeak and felt her hand go slack.

The noise of the water became distant, and everything in front of True suddenly appeared as if it was in a tunnel, and she was rushing backward. Away from the curtain of water and away from the massive aliens. Then it went dark.

TWENTY-ONE

The sound of blood pounding in his ears almost overpowered the rumble of the Kronock ship that hovered over the jungle, its green searchlight sweeping the treetops. Looking for them, Varden knew.

He and Kos had been running through the heavy undergrowth, following the flash of the alien's dark braid that swung above them as he leapt from tree to tree, his tail often gripping a branch for balance. They were going back to the village and back to the spot where the Kronock ship seemed to be focusing its search.

Varden's gut churned, but he forced himself not to think of True and what might be happening. He'd never met the scaly creatures face-to-face, but he'd heard about the Kronock for his entire life. Only recently had their enemy ventured close enough for him to get a glimpse at their new battleships—menacing gray monstrosities with the same scale-like hull as the ship now searching this planet.

He balled his hands into fists as he ran, batting away vines and branches, ignoring the sharp sting as stray leaves slapped his face and bare chest. Kos's heavy breathing reminded him that his first officer was right behind him, and this gave him a small sense of comfort. If he was going to face down the Kronock, at least he wasn't going to do it alone.

The alien overhead paused, cupping a hand to one ear, then pivoting and heading in a slightly different direction. Varden also hesitated. Was the alien still going to the village where he'd left True and Cerise? He cursed himself for not being able to speak the strange language, but he kept following. He'd learned that he didn't know the jungle well enough to venture out without a guide—or a well-marked trail—and now was not the time he wanted to be lost and wandering.

The ship glided closer to them, and Varden swallowed hard. He could smell the acrid scent of burning fuel that, along with the roar of the engine, marred the usual serenity of the jungle planet. It looked like wherever they were going was right into the belly of the beast. Good. If that was where True was, that was where he wanted to be. No *grekking* way was he letting her be taken captive by the Kronock.

The native they were following dropped to the ground and disappeared through a tall copse of trees. Varden raced forward, hoping they hadn't lost him, and almost plunged into the water.

He stumbled back and slammed into Kos, who let out a whoosh of air and fell onto his ass.

"What the...?" Kos said, lying in a tangle of green vines.

Varden extended a hand and yanked the Drexian to his feet. "Sorry. I didn't know we were coming to the waterfall."

The Kronock ship was so loud, he hadn't noticed the sound of water flowing down into the shimmering blue pool. He scanned the area for the alien who'd been leading them and saw him on the far bank, pointing to the waterfall itself and chattering loudly.

A wave of relief went through him. True had come to their place to hide. "That's my clever girl."

"They're behind there," he said to Kos, who was still picking bits of foliage from his hair.

Slipping into the water, he waded across with his first officer right behind him. He paused before going underneath the pouring water, squinting to see if he could see shapes behind the cascade. He couldn't.

Varden closed his eyes and stepped under, swiping at his face to clear it of water. Kos was a step behind him, but soon they were both on the other side, staring down at True and Cerise.

Cerise looked both surprised and pleased as she beamed up at them, her face a riot of colorful stripes. True, however, locked her gaze on him and inhaled sharply, then her eyes rolled up into her head, and she collapsed.

He caught her before she sank into the water, her body light in his arms. He glanced at Cerise.

She shrugged, raising her voice to be heard over the rushing water. "We thought you might be Kronock."

Varden scooped his woman up into his arms. He knew they should probably wait under the falls until the Kronock threat was gone, but he also needed to make sure True was fine. He couldn't do that crammed in a small space behind a waterfall.

"Stay here," he ordered Kos, cutting his eyes to Cerise to indicate he should watch the Perogling.

Without waiting for his first officer's response, Varden ducked under the water again, shielding True with his body as he curled her up into his chest. They burst back out into the pool, steam rising from the water and droplets spraying across the surface. When he'd waded to the edge, Varden placed True gently on the ground, not even bothering to get out of the water himself.

Tipping his head up, he noticed that the Kronock ship had moved away from them. Even though he could still hear it, the ugly gray hull no longer blocked out the suns overhead. Good. There was still a chance the enemy wouldn't find what they were looking for and would leave.

He returned his attention to True, lowering his ear to her chest and hearing the rhythmic thud of her heartbeat. He sat back, relief flooding his body as her eyes fluttered open.

Her face broke into a slow smile. "Varden."

The way she said his name made his heart constrict. Not the way she gasped it when he was inside her, insistent and needy, but softer, the word like a caress.

He stroked the back of his fingers down her cheek. "Cinnara. I was worried about you."

Her brows creased, forming a line between her eyes. "I was worried about you. I thought you might do something stupid like try to fight off a ship full of Kronock by yourself."

He couldn't help laughing. "Not yet."

"When you and Kos came through the waterfall, I thought you were them." Her expression clouded. "I thought they'd come to take me, like they took Bridget."

He grasped her hand. "I would never let them. I would hunt them down across the galaxy until I found you again and rip the monsters limb from limb."

True propped herself up on her elbows. "That might be the sweetest thing anyone's ever said to me."

Varden captured the side of her face in his hand before lowering his mouth to hers and savoring the sweet taste of her. As she opened her mouth to him, her tongue stroking his, desire arrowed through him. He still stood waist-deep in the water, and he pulled her toward him, her arms wrapping around his neck as she sank deeper into his kiss.

He was vaguely aware that they should be focused on evading the Kronock, but he felt the need to reassure himself that she was safe and that she was his. Her soft moan spurred him on, and he fumbled with the buttons of the wet shirt between them, desperate to feel her soft breasts and suck on her pretty pink nipples. He pushed the shirt open, cupping one globe and rolling the hard point between his thumb and finger.

"So perfect," he murmured when he'd broken the kiss.

She arched into him, and his cock throbbed, begging to be released from the constraints of his pants. He hesitated, knowing that Kos and Cerise were right behind him. How long would they wait before venturing from behind the water?

A thundering explosion jerked his attention to the sky, and the ground trembled. True sat up, her eyes no longer half-lidded with desire.

"What was that?" she asked, tugging her shirt closed.

Where the Kronock ship had been, there was now a roiling ball of fire with a black cloud of smoke billowing over it. Birds darted through the air away from the blast, and shards of the ship's shattered hull fell from the sky.

"The enemy ship exploded," he said, half to True and half to Kos, who'd burst out from under the waterfall, pulling Cerise behind him, and was now wading over to the edge.

"Did the natives do this?" Kos asked, disbelief tinging his voice.

"How?" Varden asked. "They have no advanced technology. Spears couldn't do something like this. Maybe the ship was damaged internally."

"Or maybe it was them." Cerise pointed to another ship approaching from the side.

Varden's pulse quickened as he felt a flush of pride. The second ship was black and sleek and carried all the hallmarks of a Drexian fighter.

"Yes!" Kos slammed a fist into the water, sending droplets into the air. "Our Drexian brothers have found us."

"We're rescued?" True asked.

Varden looked at the joyful expression on her face. Although he shared in her happiness, a part of him wished she was not so eager to be saved. *This is what you expected*, he reminded himself. *It couldn't last forever.*

As the Drexian ship glided toward them, the pit in his stomach returned, this time settling cold and hard. He knew that the idyllic time with the woman of his dreams had come to an end.

CHAPTER
TWENTY-TWO

"True?"

She spun around in the clearing at the top of the planet's highest point, baffled by the voice she recognized so well. Since Varden and Kos had left their only communication device transmitting on the small hill, they'd all hurried to it, so the Drexians would know where to find them. Scanning the thick jungle would take time, and no one wanted to take the chance of more Kronock ships showing up.

It hadn't bothered her that she and Varden hadn't held hands during the walk through the jungle, since they were in such a rush, but when they'd stood waiting for the Drexians to disembark from their two ships, she'd been overcome by a rush of nerves, stepping closer to him to feel his body heat. He'd glanced down at her, his finger brushing against the back of her hand, when she'd heard the loud voice.

Her head snapped up. "Ella?"

Her best friend from the station barreled down the ramp of one of the Drexian ships before it had completely lowered, her dark curls flying behind her as she ran. "We found you. I can't believe we found you."

She threw her arms around True, almost knocking her over when she reached her.

True hugged her back. "I can't believe you're part of the rescue party." She thought for a moment. "Correction. I can believe it."

"She insisted." Dakar, her tall Drexian mate with dark hair he wore pulled up into a messy man bun, followed her off the ship, shaking his head. "As in, refused to let us leave unless she was on the ship."

That sounded like Ella, True thought, smiling at her friend.

Ella held her out at arm's length and studied her. "You look good, all things considered. Really good." She raised an eyebrow and glanced down at Cerise, giving the woman a wink. "You two didn't stumble onto the fountain of youth, did you?"

"Not exactly," Cerise said, looking like a cat with canary feathers poking out of her mouth.

True shot her a look and hoped the Perogling would keep quiet until she could tell Ella everything in her own way and her own time.

"I'm not even going to ask what you're wearing," Ella said, fanning herself with one hand. "Is this place always so hot and humid?"

"It's steamier in the jungle," Cerise said.

Ella cut her eyes to Varden and Kos. "Looks like you were in good hands. The captain of the Boat, no less." Ella's eyes wandered to his bare chest, and the corners of her mouth twitched. "Less formally attired than usual."

Varden gave her a small bow. "We have had to adapt as best we could."

Ella's eyes rested on Kos next. "I can see that."

Dakar approached Varden, giving him a chest salute. "We couldn't detect a signal from your ship."

"After we crashed, it became submerged in a sinkhole of some kind. The beacon was disabled, as well as all the electrical systems."

Dakar shook his head. "That explains it."

"How did you find us then?" Varden asked, pivoting to face Dakar and Kos.

"I have to give credit to Torven," Dakar said.

A fierce-looking Drexian with shaggy hair and dark stubble on his cheeks strode down the ramp of the second ship to join them. "Since we couldn't track the ship, we decided to track the enemy who was also searching for you. We suspected you were the last one off the station, and we thought the Kronock might have gotten a bead on you. At least, they probably knew where to search. So we homed in on their movements. When one of their ships got interested in this planet, so did we."

"Old Inferno Force tactic," Dakar told him.

Varden thumped a hand on the warrior's back. "Your timing was perfect."

Torven glanced down at Kos's and Varden's attire then over his shoulders his gaze landing on True in nothing but the captain's soaking wet uniform shirt. "Did we interrupt something?"

True's cheeks warmed, but before either she or Varden could explain, Kos said, "The Kronock were homing in on us, so we were hiding beneath a waterfall. I don't know how much longer we could have evaded them."

Ella swept her arms wide. "Look at the planet, guys. They've been surviving in a jungle for days. I'm surprised they're wearing as much clothing as they are. I might be running around in a loincloth by now."

Dakar grinned at her, the hungry look in his eyes unmistakable. "Maybe I should arrange for us to get stranded here then."

Ella walked over to her mate and gave him a playful shove. "Not on your life." She held out one of her curls. "Look at how the heat is frizzing my hair already. If I were here for much longer, I'd barely be able to fit my head back in the ship."

Dakar pulled her close to him. "I like your hair when it gets wild." He lowered his voice. "Just like I like you when you get wild."

Cerise giggled. Usually such a display would have made True

uncomfortable, but now it only made her want to sidle up to Varden and feel his big arm around her waist.

Torven cleared his throat and narrowed his eyes at Dakar. "All right. Not all of us have mates on this mission."

"Sorry," Dakar said, not looking sorry at all.

"I'm assuming you're ready to depart, Captain?" Torven asked.

"Affirmative." Varden's voice was no-nonsense. "There is nothing left to recover."

"Wait," Cerise cried as the Drexians headed for the ships. "Aren't we going to say good-bye to the natives?"

True followed the woman's gaze to the nearby treetops, where dozens of the slight green aliens were balancing on branches and clutching trunks.

"Whoa," Dakar said, his hand going to the blaster on his belt.

"They're friendly," True said, quickly. "They let us sleep in their village and helped us hide from the Kronock."

Torven looked to Varden, who nodded. "We might not have survived without them."

Cerise walked to the trees, peering up and saying something in the alien language. The aliens responded with a torrent of chirpy sounds so that it sounded almost like a song.

"They're kind of cute," Ella whispered to True. "And I think they like our little Perogling friend."

The alien True had always assumed was the leader of the group swooped down to the ground, landing noiselessly and bowing low at Cerise's feet. He took her hand in his and wrapped his tail around her shoulders, saying something with an earnest expression.

"Is he proposing?" Ella asked.

"No," True said, then cocked her head to one side. "Actually, I don't know."

The alien unwound his tail and returned Cerise's hand, then raised a hand in farewell to the rest of them. Varden gave him a chest salute, and True waved.

When Cerise walked back to stand next to True, her eyes were glistening.

"Are you okay?" True asked.

Cerise nodded. "If I ever get bored on the Boat, I can always return here and rule as their queen."

"Wow," True said. "You made quite an impression."

"They said you could be my attendant," Cerise told her with a giggle.

"Until they get indoor plumbing, that's a hard no from me," True said. "I'm happy to go back to my regular life, thank you very much."

Varden cleared his throat. "Shall we?" He stepped back to let everyone walk ahead, but True hesitated.

"It feels strange to leave," she said, her voice low as they walked behind everyone else toward the two ships. "I'll miss our waterfall."

He nodded, but his face remained impassive.

True looked down at her feet, afraid to meet his eyes. "So what happens now?"

"We join the rest of the residents of the Boat," he said, not turning as they walked. "And get back to our regular lives."

She felt stung. Had he misinterpreted her throwaway comment as something more? She hadn't meant she wanted to go back to the way things were with him. Had she?

Things had been amazing with Varden, and she felt a magnetic pull to him, but she'd never imagined herself taking a Drexian mate, much less the captain of the entire Boat. What would life with him even look like? Clearly, she wouldn't be able to stay on the independent side of the station, and that had been the only home she'd known since she'd been abducted from Earth.

"True." He stopped, reaching out and touching her arm to stop her. "Neither of us planned for this to happen. You never wanted to be a tribute bride, and I, well, I never intended to have one. Maybe we should—"

"That's fine." She cut him off before he could say any more. Her eyes burned, and she prayed the tears wouldn't fall. "I get it. It was fun while it lasted, right?"

He clamped his mouth shut, and she rushed ahead before he could say anything else, catching up to Ella and looping her arm through hers on one side and Cerise's on the other.

She didn't look behind her, but she knew once they'd boarded the ship that Varden and Kos had taken the other shuttle with Torven instead of the one with her.

She'd known the risks, she told herself as she settled into a seat on the transport and strapped herself in. He'd had years to take a tribute bride, and he never had. There had to be a reason, and the reason was clearly that he had no intention of having a mate. As much as he'd talked about claiming her and her being his, it was just talk. She wasn't his. She wasn't anybody's.

True pressed her eyes shut to keep from crying, then drew in a full breath. And she never would be.

CHAPTER
TWENTY-THREE

Varden watched the other Drexian transport ship lift off the planet, his chest constricting in physical pain. He flopped down in a seat next to Kos as Torven and another officer prepared their ship for take-off. He was glad to be back in a Drexian vessel. The cool black interior felt comforting after days in the steamy jungle with unfamiliar sounds and smells. He leaned his head back against the headrest and closed his eyes, trying not to think about True but seeing nothing but images of her swirling through his mind.

How had that gone so wrong? He hadn't meant to suggest they go back to the way things had been—not completely, at least—but then she'd been so eager to latch on to the idea. He was going to suggest they keep things between them quiet for a while longer, but now the concept seemed absurd.

Had he really expected her to sneak around with him? For how long? On the planet, it had seemed like the easiest thing to do, but once they were back with everyone else, did he really expect to carry on a secret relationship with one of the independent humans and think no one would find out?

He was the captain of the Boat. Every Drexian on the station knew him by sight. Being seen with one of the human women who'd rejected being part of the tribute bride program would do more than raise a few eyebrows. It would be all anyone would talk about. He knew it would not be long until word reached High Command, and he would have to explain himself and his intentions. And what were his intentions?

If he was being honest, all he wanted was to stay in bed with True until both of them were too exhausted to move. He'd been telling her the truth when he said he'd never seriously considered taking a mate. Until now. Now, all he could think about was being with her forever. But did he have the right to claim one so young? Now that she was no longer timid and terrified, she might want to explore her options.

Maybe she was right about going their separate ways. It was probably the best idea. He couldn't keep ignoring the fact that he was twice her age. What business did he have with a human female, even one who wasn't a tribute bride? He was too old to start a family. Wasn't he?

The idea of children stirred something in him, and Varden swallowed hard. He was the captain of the Boat, a position and honor he'd worked hard to reach. He'd made plenty of sacrifices to rise to a command level, and a family didn't figure into any of that. Females were a distraction he'd never wanted and that he still couldn't afford. He spent long hours on the bridge, and he knew from other Drexians that mates required lots of time and attention. Time that, now they were leaving the alien planet, he didn't have.

He gave his head a small shake. No, the time in his life for a mate and family had passed. He would have to get over whatever feelings he had for True and let her find a young Drexian who could give her all those things. But the thought of her—his beautiful, perfect True —with another warrior made him ball his hands into fists on his lap, fury rising like bile in his throat.

"Captain?"

He opened his eyes and looked over at Kos. "Yes?"

Kos furrowed his brow. "You were growling, sir. Loudly. Is everything all right?"

Varden shifted, relaxing his fists and wiping his clammy palms on his pants, although they were also damp, so it didn't do much good. "Thinking about the Kronock."

Kos nodded. "Understood."

Varden looked out the front of the ship and saw that they had cleared the ship's atmosphere. He unstrapped himself, eager not to be sitting. "Is there a status update on the Boat?"

Torven swiveled around to face him. "Affirmative, Captain. Inferno Force arrived with reinforcements shortly after you left. The station sustained damage, but nothing that can't be repaired. Our forces were able to destroy half of the Kronock battleships, enough to send them scrambling to regroup."

"And an Earth invasion?" Varden asked. Although he'd never set foot on the planet, he'd been living in its solar system for half of his life, and he had a fondness for the little blue ball.

Torven grinned, cracking his knuckles and shaking his head. "They abandoned that plan when our forces surrounded them and cut them off from a direct path. We positioned two of our Inferno Force battleships on the dark side of Earth's moon as a defensive measure, but they didn't even make the attempt."

Varden felt his shoulders relax. "That's good news. Where are the Kronock now?"

"We tracked them back to their own territory, aside from the ship looking for you and a few others. We suspect they were trying to pick off some of our escape shuttles."

Varden folded his arms across his chest and frowned. Sounded like the Kronock. "And all the residents of the Boat made it to the rendezvous point?"

The grin slid off Torven's face. "Obviously, not your ship. There's one other that hadn't checked in when Dakar and I left to search for you. We suspected a malfunction with the ship's jump drive had caused the delay. Dorn took a crew to check on them."

"How many aboard the missing ship?" he asked.

"We're not certain. There was quite a bit of chaos when we all abandoned ship. From initial manifests, it appears to be four humans, one Gatazoid, one Vexling, and two Drexian pilots."

"Four humans?"

Torven's face contorted into a grimace. "The new tribute brides and their handlers, sir."

"*Grek.*" Varden barely whispered the word. They'd only recently resumed transporting tribute brides from Earth, and he knew the women Torven mentioned were the entirety of the first of the new arrivals. "I'm assuming they were out of stasis?"

"They'd all gone through their medical procedures and been placed in fantasy suites. Serge and Reina had even started working with one of the women when we got word of the attack. They managed to get all their charges into one transport and escape the ship unscathed."

"And then?" Varden prompted.

Torven's gaze darted to the floor. "We lost contact, sir. But like I said, we suspect their jump drive malfunctioned. We have no evidence the Kronock intercepted them. When I was leaving to search for you, Dorn was leaving with his search party."

Varden rubbed a hand over his forehead. "At least Dorn is on it. That Drexian never gives up."

Torven clasped both hands behind his back so that his chest puffed out. "He *is* Inferno Force. We never accept defeat."

Varden was glad the fierce, slightly wild warriors were on his side. "I'm grateful you didn't give up on finding us."

The other Drexian at the controls turned to look at them. "Prepare to jump."

Torven dropped back into his seat, and Varden did the same.

Kos strode into the cockpit wearing a clean gray standard-issue shirt. He handed one to Varden. "I thought you might not want to return to your command bare-chested."

Varden couldn't help smiling at the idea of giving orders shirtless. "You thought correctly." He tugged the shirt over his head before fastening the seat straps across his shoulders.

Torven held up a hand. "Three...two...one...jump."

Varden felt a pull from the center of his stomach as the ship jumped to the new coordinates. Within the span of a heartbeat, the view out the front of the ship changed. Instead of the vastness of space, he could see what appeared to be a moon of some kind. To both sides, Drexian battleships hovered above the surface.

"And we're back to the rendezvous point," Torven said, standing. "The Drexian colony on Graxos."

Even though Varden couldn't see the buildings he knew covered the surface, he also knew how many hundreds of residents there had been on the Boat. "You sure there's room for a few more?"

"It's cozy, but I'm sure we'll manage." Torven winked as he headed out of the cockpit. "Perhaps there is someone you wouldn't mind sharing quarters with?"

Varden cursed to himself. He hadn't even been able to hide his feelings from Torven. This did not bode well for returning to life as usual.

"Sir?" the Drexian remaining at the console called out, and both he and Torven spun around.

"Yes?" Torven lingered in the doorway, clearly anxious to leave.

"The other ship that was traveling in tandem with us?" the officer said as his fingers tapped away on the flat display.

"Dakar's ship," Torven said.

And True's ship, Varden thought.

"It's no longer with us, sir." The Drexian swiveled around. "It didn't make the jump."

"Impossible." Torven crossed back to the console in two long strides. "That ship was fully functional. Have you sent a message to their coordinates?"

The Drexian nodded. "No response, sir. Long-range scanners show they are no longer at those coordinates."

"Where the *grek* are they?" Torven yelled, pounding his fist against the nearest wall.

Varden felt frozen to his seat, even as fear made his body tremble.

Where was True?

CHAPTER
TWENTY-FOUR

True put a hand to her head. Why did it hurt so much? She opened her eyes tentatively, wincing as flashing red lights assaulted her. She put a hand up to shield her eyes from the bright warning lights coming from the ship's console, wishing she could make the alarms stop shrieking.

She glanced to Cerise, who was strapped into the seat next to hers in the cockpit. The Perogling looked unconscious, her head slumped to one side and her wig hanging on for dear life. They'd taken seats behind the pilots, while Ella had gone to the back of the ship to retrieve her tablet.

The last thing she remembered was the pilot giving them a countdown for the jump, but instead of ending up at the Drexian rendezvous point, they'd jumped right in front of an alien ship. Before Dakar could jump away, they'd been fired on. That's why the sirens were going off, she thought. They'd been attacked.

Peering out the front of the ship, she saw the attacking ship. She wasn't an expert on all things Kronock, but it didn't look like the scaly-armored ship that had hovered over them on the jungle planet. This ship looked like it had been assembled in a junkyard— the hull was a collection of various colored metals and most of it was dented and rusted. She gave her head a shake as she breathed in the smell of char. How had a bucket of bolts like *that* disabled a Drexian ship?

She unhooked her safety straps and attempted to stand, but a hard jolt almost knocked her over. What was that? A grinding noise made her look toward the center of the ship, then she heard the sound of scraping and a pop as a hatch opened.

Her mouth went dry. They were being boarded. She looked desperately around the cockpit. Dakar and the other Drexian were still passed out or dead, blood trickling down their faces. Shit, shit, shit. She had no idea where Ella was—if she was knocked out in the back of the ship or if she was hiding. She wished with all her heart that she'd taken the same transport as Varden. If only he was here right now, she wouldn't feel so scared.

Why had she been so cold to him when they'd parted? *Because you didn't think it might be the last time you'd see him,* she told herself, hearing the loud thunk of boots hitting metal.

"How could I have known we'd be attacked by aliens?" she muttered to herself, her eyes scouring the space for a hiding place. She pressed her hand against a few of the black curved panels inset in the walls, but they were small cubbies. She cursed as she realized the compact space held no secret compartments large enough for her.

The footfalls were heavy as they approached her. She gave a final look at the Drexians, who were still unmoving. She was afraid to touch them and see if they were dead. She didn't want to know if they were. It was too awful, especially if her best friend's mate was dead. She fumbled with the blaster at his waist, holding it out as an enormous creature stepped into the cockpit.

True felt her knees start to buckle, but she forced herself to stand up tall. The alien blocking the entrance was as tall as a Drexian, but with rust-colored flesh that seemed to be melting off his body. Rolls of it hung from his jowls and below the pointed tusks jutting out of his face. His black eyes were beady and almost buried in his wrinkled skin. He had no visible neck, and he appeared to be nearly as wide as he was tall, with arms that were as thick as telephone poles. A dull patchwork of armor covered his torso, but it seemed to be cobbled together from different metals and animal skins.

A hodge-podge, just like his ship, True thought.

His eyes went to the blaster in her shaking hand, and quicker than she could have imagined, he batted it out of her hand.

"You will come with me," he barked.

Her translator decoded his words, but it sounded like he spoke with a mouthful of marbles, the syllables a harsh jumble.

Backing up, her legs hit Dakar's seat, but he didn't stir. Cerise, however, looked up and emitted a tiny squeak as she saw the alien towering over her.

"Raith-Kan," she said, spitting out the words as if they were a curse.

"You know him?" she asked her friend.

Cerise shook her head, her face grim. "I know of his kind."

Well, that wasn't reassuring.

The Raith-Kan glanced down and grinned, revealing black, toothless gums. "A Perogling. You'll fetch a nice price."

"We belong to the Drexian empire," True said, hoping to stall him in case Varden had realized they were missing and was seconds away from swooping in and rescuing them. "You don't want to harm us."

The creature laughed, drool dripping down his chin. "Why would I harm you when I can sell you to Kvasiron and get enough credits to live like an emperor?"

True noticed that Cerise's usually iridescent blue skin had paled.

"Who is Kvasiron?" she whispered, not taking her eyes off the disgusting alien.

"Not who," Cerise said. "*What.* Kvasiron is a notorious prison planet that also deals in the slave trade. We do *not* want to end up there."

True's throat felt like sandpaper as she attempted to swallow. She felt like crying, but she did not want to show weakness. "If you take us, it will be considered an act of war against the Drexians. You do not want them on your bad side."

She didn't know if it would technically be considered an act of war, but she was pretty sure the Drexians wouldn't mind her taking a little creative license.

The massive alien hesitated then curled his lip. "They will never find you. And once you are on Kvasiron, there is nothing even the mighty Drexians can do. Not against the Vrex. No one escapes from the prison guards on Kvasiron."

A shiver went down her spine. That didn't sound good. She did not want to meet these Vrex in person.

"You're making a big mistake," she said, in a last ditch attempt to talk the Raith-Kan out of taking them or to give the Drexians more time to reach them.

"I don't think so," he said, lifting Cerise out of her chair as if she was a doll, her straps falling in strips to the floor. He tucked her under one arm then reached for True.

She knew she was out of her league, but no way was she going down without a fight. She dove for the blaster, almost closing her fingers around it, before she was snatched up and shoved under his other arm, her arms pinned tightly to her sides.

Struggling in his choking grip, True had to duck her head so as not to hit the doorway as he trudged back to the middle of the ship. The sensation of being held by his sagging flesh was almost as repulsive as the stench coming off his body. She pressed her lips together so as not to gag.

She felt herself being hoisted up and through the overhead hatch—into the arms of an equally disgusting and smelly Raith-Kan. This one seemed even less friendly, if that was possible, and he immediately clamped irons onto her wrists and shoved her to the floor.

Pain shot through her legs as she landed on her bare knees, feeling them scrape on the hard steel. Cerise landed next to her moments later, falling on her side and rolling. Before she could ask her friend if she was okay, they were both lifted to their feet and dragged along behind the surly alien.

The Raith-Kan ship was as dingy on the inside as it was on the outside. Lights flickered, casting a yellow glow on the exposed wires dangling from above and the uneven patches of metal welded to the walls. The plodding steps of the Raith-Kan echoed as they walked; the only other noises were the uneven hum of the ship's engine and the sound of garbled alien chatter.

They passed several more hulking aliens with rolls of flesh and sharp tusks, but even though True didn't make eye contact, she could feel their gazes following her. She could make out a few words as they whispered to each other.

Pale one. Small one. Fuck them both.

She told herself to ignore them. They were going to sell her. Not rape her. At least, she hoped not. The thought of those rolls of flesh touching her made her want to retch.

They reached a cell with bars. She and Cerise were pushed inside, and the door slammed shut with a loud clang. She caught herself before she fell, and she helped Cerise up off the floor.

"Assholes," she said under her breath, brushing the grime off Cerise's clothes. "At least they put us together."

"It won't be for long," Cerise said. "As soon as we get to Kvas-iron, they'll split us up. I'll sell quickly. They won't know what to do with you."

"I don't know if that's a good thing or a bad thing."

Cerise didn't blink. "A bad thing."

"Oh." She glanced around. The cell sat in the center of a larger room—she guessed it was the center of the ship—and it was linked with three other cells to form a large square. All of the other cells were empty. There were two guards slouching against a far door. "It doesn't matter. The Drexians will come for us before that happens."

Cerise gave her a weary smile. "The Raith-Kan were right. Once they get us to the prison planet, there's no escape until we're sold. Or we die. No one gets off Kvasiron."

True sat down hard, the reality of the situation hitting her. She wanted to believe that Varden would come for her, but he had no idea where she was or who'd taken her. Everyone else on the Drexian ship was either dead or unconscious.

She pressed the heels of her hands against her eyes as tears spilled down her cheeks. She was never going to see Varden again, and the last thing she'd said to him was something flippant about it having been fun. She hated that she'd said that and confirmed what he probably already thought—that she was too young and silly for someone as important as him. Why hadn't she just told him the truth—that she couldn't imagine her life without him in it?

The Raith-Kan shipped jerked as it accelerated, taking them away from the Drexian ship and their best chance at rescue.

Well, it's too late now.

CHAPTER
TWENTY-FIVE

"We have to go back." Varden leapt from his seat. After being immobile with terror, he now felt compelled to act—and fast.

The Drexian at the ship's console stared at him. "Go back to where we were? But they're gone." He dropped his gaze. "Sir."

Torven eyed the captain, then nodded. "I agree. We have to do something. My best friend and his mate are also on that ship." He crossed his arms over his chest. "But the best way to find them might not be to go back to where we jumped from. If they didn't make it here, but they're no longer there, their jump must have either malfunctioned or been misdirected."

"Misdirected?" Kos asked, standing next to his captain.

"It's something we saw occasionally in Inferno Force. The most ruthless bounty hunters and raiders have technology that could misdirect ships in mid-jump."

"You think...?" He couldn't finish his question. The thought of True being intercepted by bounty hunters or raiders was not a happy one.

Torven gave a half-shrug as he fingered the black craktow tooth dangling in the hollow of his throat. "It's a possibility. It's also possible that the ship glitched, although that ship was checked over recently by my mate."

Varden knew that the Drexian warrior's mate, Trista, was a skilled mechanic. He'd heard that all the pilots wanted her to check over their ships before they flew. "So it likely *wasn't* a malfunction, then."

Torven didn't respond. The captain knew that neither of them wanted to admit the possibilities.

"Scan the jump path for signs of the vessel," Varden said to the officer at the console, then pulled out a small device and began tapping on it. "If they were jerked out of a jump, they'd be between us and the point of origin somewhere."

The Drexian spun back around, his fingers flying across the console as Varden watched, a sick feeling washing over him. What an idiot he'd been. He never should have let her leave the alien planet without telling her exactly how much he cared for her.

He flashed back to her striding off onto the other ship, her head held high. Of course she hadn't looked back at him. He'd just told her he'd never intended to take a mate and neither had she. She'd obviously taken it to mean he thought what they'd had was nothing more than a fling, when nothing could be further from the truth. Not that he'd bothered to explain that to her. He'd let her walk up that ramp, convincing himself it was for the best when he'd felt his heart breaking. And now she might be in danger.

"Fool," he said to himself, and the Drexian at the console looked briefly over his shoulder. Varden cleared his throat to cover his slip. "Any luck, Officer?"

"Actually, Captain, I think I've found them."

Varden almost threw his arms around the warrior. "Truly? Then set a course for that location."

"Are we jumping?" The officer looked between him and Torven. Varden knew the young Drexian must be torn. He was the captain of the Boat, yet Torven was the captain of the vessel they were on.

Varden knew he should defer to Torven. He pivoted to face him. "Do we have enough power?"

Torven made a single, curt movement with his head. "We may have to take the long way back, but let's jump in. I want to know what happened out there, and why they're so off-course."

Varden let out a relieved breath, giving Torven a grateful smile. He collapsed back in his seat and strapped in for the jump, able to breathe easier now that they'd located True's ship.

"I'm sure she is fine, sir," Kos said, his voice hushed so that the other two Drexians couldn't hear.

Varden glanced over at his first officer, his cheeks warming. Maybe this was the first step in admitting his feelings for the human. "Thank you, Kos. I'm sure you're right, but I'm still worried."

Kos's usually serious expression lightened, and he gave the captain a smile and a nod. "Understood."

"Jumping in three...two...one." The Drexian in the pilot's chair held up his fist as Torven took the other seat in front of the console. "Jumping."

Varden felt the familiar tug that pushed him back in the seat, then he was released, and the other Drexian ship had materialized in front of them. Unhooking himself, he stood so he could lean closer to the view screen.

"The ship looks undamaged," Torven said. "Hailing them."

"Scanning for life signs," his officer said, tilting his head at the read-out. "That's odd."

"What's odd?" Varden asked.

"I have life signs, but not as many as I should." He tapped the screen again. "No. My readings are consistent. One human and two Drexians."

"One human?" Varden's flicker of hope was spluttering. He knew there had been two humans on board, not to mention the Perogling, Cerise.

"No Peroglings?" Kos asked, as if reading his mind. He now

stood shoulder to shoulder next to Varden, and the captain found the Drexian's presence comforting.

"Negative. No Peroglings."

"No answer to my hails, either," Torven said, his voice a growl. "But they *are* alive in there. At least some of them."

"I'm picking up something else unusual," the other Drexian said. "Some sort of fuel leak."

Varden squinted as he peered at the black-hulled ship. "They're leaking fuel?" He thought of their propulsion technology. Was that even possible?

"That's what's so unusual. It's not coming from the Drexian ship, because it isn't the type of fuel we use. It's a cruder, fossil fuel."

"So where did it come from?" Kos asked.

Torven stood suddenly, causing Varden to step back. "We won't know anything until we get over there. I don't have any idea what condition Dakar is in, but if he isn't answering my hails, he isn't conscious."

"I'm coming with you," Varden said.

"I, as well," Kos added.

Torven raised an eyebrow, but he didn't object. He merely flicked his gaze to the Drexian still seated at the console. "You've got the bridge, Jovak."

As they started out of the cockpit, a voice made Torven jerk to a stop.

"Dakar to Torven. Are you there, brother?"

Torven lunged for the console, pressing the button to transmit. "I'm here. Are you all right? What happened?"

Dakar breathed heavily for a few moments before answering. "I'm fine, I think. My officer needs medical attention, but he should be okay. I'm still piecing together what happened. We were mid-jump when we suddenly dropped out and were fired upon, but it was some sort of energy weapon that stunned us."

"Your ship appears to have minimal damage," Torven told him.

"I remember it disabled our shields and weapons before we could do anything, and the next thing I know, Ella's shaking me."

Torven glanced at Varden. "So Ella is the human who survived?"

Varden's blood ran cold, and he gripped the back of the nearest chair.

"Everyone survived, Torv." Dakar's voice vibrated with anger. "It was the Raith-Kan. They took True and Cerise."

"I was in the back of the ship when we jumped." Ella's shaky voice came over the transmission. "I got knocked out like everyone else, and when I came to, I heard that someone had boarded the ship. I crept out and saw them dragging True and Cerise off." She choked back a sob. "There was nothing I could do. They were huge, and I didn't have any weapons with me. I was afraid if I revealed myself then there would be no one to go after them." Another muffled sob. "I thought they'd already killed Dakar and our pilot."

"You did the right thing," Torven assured her, even as he scraped a hand through his loose hair. "At least we know who took them. That's a start."

"And we know *where* they took them," Dakar said, hesitating before he spoke again. "Kvasiron."

"*Grek.*" Torven put both hands to his head. "Not the Vrex."

Varden thought his knees might give way, but he forced himself to take a deep breath. Even though he captained a space station far from the prison planet, the place was notorious, and the Vrex who guarded it were both legendary and infamous. "Were True and Cerise unhurt when they were taken?"

"They looked fine," Ella said, then let out a mirthless laugh. "True was fighting like hell."

That's my girl, Varden thought. *You're tougher than everyone thinks.*

"We need to get them back before the Raith-Kan get them to Kvasiron," Dakar said. "Once they're inside…"

"Agreed," Torven said. "How many Raith-Kan ships were there?"

"Only one, as far as I could tell. It all happened pretty fast."

"The Raith-Kan couldn't have gotten far," Varden said. "And if they're leaving a trail of crud, they might not be too hard to chase down."

Torven wrinkled his nose. "It's been a while since I've battled the Raith-Kan." He punched a fist into his open palm. "I look forward to showing those junkyard dogs what happens to those who cross the Drexians and take our females."

Varden glanced at the four warriors. "Are we enough to take them?"

Flashes outside the ship drew Varden's attention. At least three ships had just jumped in around them, all of them large and black-hulled.

"Now we are." Torven grinned. "I called for a little Inferno Force backup." He looked from one Drexian warrior to the other. "Ready to go hunting?"

Varden felt his chest swell with pride. *Hold on, True,* he thought. *We're coming.*

CHAPTER
TWENTY-SIX

True wrapped her arms around her bent legs and leaned into Cerise. They sat back to back on the floor so they wouldn't have to lean against the hard bars of the cell, but her body ached nonetheless. Her scraped knees had stopped bleeding, but her head still throbbed from being knocked out when the Raith-Kan attacked. Her only comfort was feeling her friend's steady breaths behind her.

"You're sure your arms are okay?" she asked Cerise, probably for the tenth time.

"I'm sure."

To be honest, True just needed to hear the woman's voice every so often. It beat the snuffling and snorting sounds coming from their two guards. She avoided looking at them, the sight of the sagging burnished flesh making her want to either scream or puke.

"Any idea how long it will take to get to this prison planet place?" she asked, shifting to take the weight off the side of her body that was going numb.

Cerise shivered, and True didn't know if it was a reaction to her mentioning the prison planet or because the ship wasn't heated, and cold air seemed to seep in through gaps in the patchwork walls.

"I don't know. From what little I've heard, the place isn't close to any reputable planets. Why would you want a place like that in your neighborhood?"

True found it funny to think of groupings of planets as neighborhoods, but then again, a lot of what she'd learned about alien life had taken some adjustment. If it wasn't near Drexian territory, that was good. The longer it took to get there, the better. More time for the Drexians to track them down and rescue them.

She thought about those left behind on the ship. She hoped Ella was okay, and that Dakar and the other Drexian hadn't really been dead. Even though she and Cerise had been taken, at least the Raith-Kan hadn't thought to thoroughly search the rest of the ship or make sure the Drexians were dead. That was the one silver lining to all this.

Come on Ella, she thought. *You have to be okay.*

One of the guards in the corner let out a long, wet breath, saliva dribbling down his chin. True forced herself to look away. At least the pair weren't standing any closer. The Raith-Kan clearly did not believe in bathing. Although their stench hung in the air, she knew it would be unbearable if the guards were at the bars.

"So what do you know about these Raith-Kan?" she whispered to Cerise when she saw one guard's head droop.

"Zylia never allowed them in our house on Lymora III," Cerise said with some amount of pride in her voice.

"Zylia?"

"The Valoushe madam at the pleasure house where Shreya found me. She might have been terrifying in her own way, but she had standards for her girls."

True tried to process all this. She knew Cerise had worked at a pleasure house and had helped Shreya escape, but she'd never asked for details. Before, she'd found the concept embarrassing and shocking. Now, she was more curious than anything. "So it was an upscale brothel?"

"Oh, yes." Cerise's usual animated tone had returned. "It was the ultimate in luxury. We had everything you could imagine, and we would do just about anything our clients could dream up."

True's face flushed at the thought of what wild scenarios the male visitors might have requested. "But not Raith-Kan."

"Never." Cerise lowered her voice, but the creatures in the corner didn't seem to be paying attention. "They are as stupid as they are repulsive. No pleasurer had the stomach for them. Perhaps some of the lower houses took them on."

"Have they always been slavers?" From the cluster of cells, it was clear this wasn't a one-off operation.

"They'll steal anything and sell it—weapons, cargo, medicine. I think they just happened to get lucky with us."

True attempted to swallow, but her throat was parched. "Because you're a Perogling?"

Cerise let out a small, resigned sigh. "Yes. They don't know what species you are, but they know enough to know you're small and pretty and will fetch a decent price."

"Does that mean we'll both end up in pleasure houses?" The thought terrified her. She'd only known Varden, and with him it had been special. The thought of being forced to spread her legs for scores of random aliens made bile churn in her stomach. She would rather die.

"Maybe." Cerise shrugged, her small shoulders rising and falling against True's back. "Unless a pirate ship decides they need a pleasurer to service their crew."

This just got better and better, True thought, telling herself not to cry. She rested her forehead on her crossed arms. The two guards said something to each other, their words running together and making it hard for her universal translator to work, but she got the impression that one of the Raith-Kan needed to take a leak.

When he'd left the holding area, Cerise nudged her in the ribs. "Fancy getting off this ship?"

"What?" she whispered, almost falling backward as the alien stood.

"Like I said," Cerise muttered out one side of her mouth. "These guys are very stupid."

True hopped up, watching in amazement as Cerise strutted toward the steel bars and transformed her voice into a velvet purr.

"It's too bad your bosses don't let you get a taste," she said, eyeing the Raith-Kan as if he was the most gorgeous creature she'd ever seen.

True had to force herself not to gape in utter shock. Cerise's act was so convincing that, for a moment, she almost believed that the woman was attracted to the disgusting creature.

The guard looked startled, as well. "I can't talk to the prisoners."

"Come on," Cerise chided. "No one's here but us. Your friend even left. Don't you want to come over here and visit us? I'll bet you've never had a Perogling before."

He rubbed one of his tusks and grunted. "Can you do what they say you can?"

"That and more," Cerise said, licking her lips.

"Are you sure about this?" True whispered, as the Raith-Kan advanced.

Cerise's seductive smile didn't falter as the creature reached the bars, his pungent scent preceding him and making True clamp a hand over her nose. "You'll have to come inside to get the full treatment, sweetie."

True had no idea what the Perogling's plan was, since they didn't have any weapons on them, and the huge alien was the size of both of them put together and then doubled. She backed up as the guard fumbled with the chains on the cell, finally swinging open the door and giving them both a black-gummed grin.

"I want both of you," he said, not bothering to catch the drool dripping from his lips.

"Oh, you'll get both of us, sweetie," Cerise said. "But we have to hurry. Drop your pants."

How far was Cerise going to go? True gulped and averted her eyes as the Raith-Kan unfastened his leather pants and they fell to the floor. She couldn't resist darting a glance at him, but if there was anything to see, it was hidden beneath rolls of drooping, rust-colored skin.

Cerise rubbed her hands together. "I just love a male with some fleshiness."

True took another step back. She couldn't see any weapons on the alien she could grab—no blaster or blades. Maybe he depended on his brute strength, especially when it came to guarding small females. So much for that bright idea. And his bulk still blocked the cell door. They wouldn't be getting around him. She hoped Cerise had something up her sleeve.

"First my tusks," he said, his garbled words husky.

"Of course," Cerise said, patting her hands to her big wig. "The tusks. You'll have to get on your knees for that."

He dropped onto his knees, and the floor shook. Cerise approached, stroking one of his curved tusks with her hand. As he groaned, her other hand drew a sharp pin out of her wig, and she drove it into the back of his neck, angled up.

True slapped a hand over her mouth to keep from screaming in surprise as the huge alien grunted one final time and fell forward with a loud thud.

"Come on." Cerise replaced the pin in her wig, the now-slick, shiny needle vanishing into the mass of pink curls. She beckoned True as she stepped over the dead guard's bare legs. "We need to be anywhere but here when the other one returns."

True managed to nod and follow Cerise out, even though she had the urge to retch. They ran to the door, poking their heads out and finding the corridor empty.

True pointed to the right. "I think we came from this direction."

They hurried down the corridor on tiptoes, trying to retrace the steps they'd taken when they were brought on board. It was to their advantage that the lighting was bad and there were large crates and loose panels along the way. When they heard the pounding footsteps of a Raith-Kan, they could easily duck behind something and be unnoticed as he passed.

After crouching behind a cluster of rusty barrels, True pulled Cerise to her. "I think we're going in circles. How are we going to get off this ship before they find out that we killed one of their crew members?"

"There has to be a shuttle somewhere. Ships this large always have shuttles."

True tightened her grip on Cerise's sleeve. "Have you looked around you? This thing is barely holding together."

Cerise opened her mouth to respond, but a loud wailing sound made them both cover their ears. The spluttering yellow lighting was replaced with a flashing red siren.

So much for escaping before they found the dead guard.

CHAPTER
TWENTY-SEVEN

"Confirmed," Torven said as they fired another shot at the Raith-Kan vessel and watched it rock from the impact. "One human and one Perogling inside."

Varden stood with his hands clutched behind his back so no one could see how hard he was squeezing them. "Are we sure our weapons won't tear that monstrosity in two?"

"We had to disable their weapons systems so they couldn't get off a shot." Torven peered out the front of the ship and shook his head. "Luckily, they didn't see us coming. Now we don't need to keep firing."

"So they can't return fire?" Kos asked, obviously not eager to sample the energy blast that had taken out Dakar's ship.

"Or escape," Torven added, motioning with his head to the Inferno Force ships that surrounded the rusty ship.

"Remind me to thank your Inferno Force brothers after this," Varden said.

"Trust me, they're happy to do it. It's always a good day when you take out a Raith-Kan ship."

Varden tried not to sound as desperate as he felt. "I'd like to lead the boarding party."

Torven's mouth twitched for a scant moment before he nodded. "Of course, Captain." He tapped the console, bringing them closer to the enemy ship, and finally lowering them over its top hatch. The Drexian ship jerked as it locked on to the Raith-Kan vessel.

Torven touched a hand to the blaster on his waist and turned, meeting Kos's eyes.

"I'm with you," Kos said before Varden could ask.

He swallowed the lump in his throat and nodded. His first officer fell in step, and the two Drexians strode to the center of the ship. Torven joined them as Varden opened the central hatch, leaving an open hole flush with the Raith-Kan vessel.

"Ready?" Varden asked, glancing at both men.

Torven grinned wildly, a blaster in one hand and a curved Drexian blade in another. He'd shed his uniform jacket and wore a tight black shirt that showed the tattoos down one bicep. "Always."

Varden wrenched open the battered hatch of the enemy ship, leaning back in case they were fired on from below, but there was nothing. He leapt down, landing in a crouch inside the ship, his blaster extended. Moving aside quickly, he swept the surroundings as the two other Drexians dropped down next to him.

He heard the pounding of feet and garbled screams. The ship smelled putrid, but also of smoke. Clearly, their attack had done some internal damage.

Good, he thought. These monsters didn't deserve to be left in one piece. As long as he could get True and Cerise out before it burned or blew up.

"Any idea where they could be holding our women?" Kos asked, his voice low.

"Raith-Kan usually keep live cargo in a holding pen near the middle of the ship," Torven said.

The idea of his sweet True as live cargo in a pen made Varden's blood boil. He told himself to focus on her, not his anger, even as his body shook with fury.

"This way." Torven jerked his head for them to follow him and moved down a dingy corridor. A Raith-Kan lumbered into view, and Torven dropped him with a blaster shot. He glanced back at Varden. "I assume we're okay with not providing mercy to these slave traders."

"You assume correctly," Varden growled, staring down at the alien and the rolls of rust-colored skin draping off him like a loose garment, dingy yellow tusks jutting from his face. He could only imagine how terrified True had been to be taken captive by creatures like these.

Kos tugged his sleeve, and he pulled his eyes from the dead creature, reminding himself that time was of the essence.

They moved swiftly through the ship. Red lights flashed overhead, illuminating things in bursts and making it harder to dodge the barrels and crates that cluttered the corridors. They encountered few Raith-Kan, and all were instantly felled by one of their blasters—often all three—the massive bodies landing with ominous thuds on the metal floor, orange goo leaking from them instead of blood.

Was there anything about these Raith-Kan that wasn't repulsive, wondered Varden? He was glad he'd never encountered them before. One advantage to being the captain of the Boat—he didn't have to interact with the scum of the universe. It was easy to understand why Torven relished battling them, though—killing slavers was distinctly satisfying.

Over the wail of the sirens, Varden heard yells. Although the language was strange and slurred, he could make out that the remaining Raith-Kan were shouting something about their slaves.

True, he thought, his stomach twisting.

A pair of Raith-Kan met them at the next bend, and these were faster than the previous ones they'd encountered. One of them dodged under Torven's blaster fire and tackled him around the waist. The other used the battle as a distraction, punching out and catching Kos on the side of the head. The Drexian stumbled, but Varden caught him, tucking his first officer behind him as he avoided being punched himself.

"Thief," the Raith-Kan bellowed, lunging for him and knocking him to the ground. "You will not take our prize."

The weight of the alien landing on him stunned Varden, and he barely dodged to the left in time to miss being slammed by an open fist. The creature roared again, jerking his head back to slam it into his when his eyes bugged out and he collapsed. The weight of the now-dead Raith-Kan was almost as crushing as a blow, and Varden struggled to roll the alien off of him.

Hearing more blaster fire, he hesitated, hoping it wasn't Torven he'd heard falling. Within moments, the massive alien was being pushed off him, and Torven and Kos helped him to his feet. Both Raith-Kan lay dead.

"You?" he asked, looking at the alien who'd tried to kill him, a scorch mark burned across his back, and then pointedly at Kos.

His first officer shrugged. "I was afraid his weight would kill you, but it seemed a risk you'd want me to take."

Varden almost laughed, clamping a hand on the Drexian's shoulder.

"We're close," Torven said, waving for them to join him as he reached the end of the corridor and pushed through a heavy metal door.

The large space they entered was clearly where they stored their living cargo, as four large steel cages linked in the middle could attest. Varden quickly assessed that all were empty, and there appeared to be one dead Raith-Kan and another huddled over him.

Torven raised his blaster to fire, but Varden threw out a hand.

"Wait," he said. "If our women are gone, he might know where they are."

The Raith-Kan spun as he heard sound, but Torven fired a stream of blaster fire at the hand that reached for his weapon.

"I wouldn't try that if I were you," Torven told him, advancing on the enemy fighter.

Varden scanned the area more thoroughly. No sign of True and Cerise. He wanted to scream with frustration.

"Where are the women you took?" he asked, aiming his own blaster at the Raith-Kan's head.

"They are ours." The creature spat out the words. "Get your own slaves to sell."

It took all of Varden's self-control not to drop the creature instantly, but he knew they needed him. His information, at least. "They were here, yes? Where are they now? Did you move them when we attacked you? Where are you hiding them?"

The Raith-Kan scowled at him.

"We will find them. It's only a matter of time. If you don't want us to kill every soul on board, you'll tell me now."

The alien narrowed his eyes, then started to laugh, his flab quivering as his entire body shook. Varden exchanged a glance with Torven, who looked as perplexed as him.

"They were more trouble than they were worth," the Raith-Kan finally said, swiping at a ribbon of spit dangling from his mouth. "We don't have them anymore."

Grek. Had they already offloaded the women or had they sold them along the way to more traders?

"Did you sell them to other slave traders?" Varden asked.

The alien's gaze went to his dead comrade, and his expression hardened. "They killed one of us, so we got rid of them."

Torven stepped closer. "Got rid of them?"

The Raith-Kan's face broke into a menacing, black-gummed smile. "Put them out the airlock."

Varden took a moment to process what the creature had said, aware that both Drexians were looking at him. Blood roared in his ears.

Impossible. She couldn't be dead. Not after all this. Not after they'd tracked her across the galaxy. Not after he'd finally found her.

Before he could think better of it, Varden fired at the alien's arm, wounding him and causing him to fall to the side. Then he was on the Raith-Kan, raining punches on the injured creature, both of their screams of agony echoing off the cold steel of the room and reverberating in his chest.

CHAPTER
TWENTY-EIGHT

True huddled behind a large metal crate, with Cerise kneeling below her. The screaming sirens made her already-sore head ache even more, and she wished they would turn off the flashing red lights. It was clear the Raith-Kan had discovered the dead body. Why else would they be running around the ship and shouting?

Shivering from shock, she watched a pair of the massive aliens thunder by, not even glancing around. If they were searching for them, the Raith-Kan weren't very good at it, although she remembered that Cerise had said they were stupid.

She wrapped her arms around herself, wishing she were anywhere but hiding on a Raith-Kan slaving ship. As much as she'd complained about how primitive the planet was that they'd crashed on, she would have given anything to be back there now. She wouldn't even mind the sticky humidity.

At the moment, the thought of the heat made her smile. Then she flashed back to being in the waterfall with Varden, the steam rising up off the water around them. She closed her eyes and sighed, almost able to picture the two of them, limbs wrapped around each other as the water cascaded behind them.

A jolt pulled her from the memory, and she braced an arm on the nearby wall for balance as the ship rocked. *What was that?*

"Do you smell smoke?" she asked Cerise, cupping a hand around her mouth and almost shouting in the tiny woman's ear.

Cerise sniffed the air and nodded. "This ship doesn't look like it's new or in great shape. Maybe they have to burn fuel."

True wanted to ask how else the ship would fly, but she held her tongue. Right now they needed to focus on staying hidden and then getting off the ship. Given enough time, she knew that even stupid aliens could find them if they didn't escape.

The ship jolted again, and Cerise grabbed her arm for balance. Both women looked at each other. If True had been in a car, she would have said they'd just gotten in a fender-bender. That was absurd, of course, because they weren't in a car and the Raith-Kan ship was flying. Or was it?

The blaring sirens made it hard to tell right away, but when she put a hand to the metal wall of the vessel, she could tell it no longer vibrated. They'd stopped. But why?

She tugged Cerise's sleeve. "The ship isn't moving."

The Perogling cocked her head to the side. "You're right."

More Raith-Kan lumbered past them, yelling at each other about fighting off someone. Clearly, they weren't talking about her and Cerise. Then, who?

She peeked her head out from their hiding place. She caught a glimpse of some burly-looking figures in the distance. Not Raith-Kan.

"I think someone else is on the ship," she whispered to Cerise. "I think the Raith-Kan are under attack."

"The question is, are the attackers better or worse than them?"

"There are worse aliens than the Raith-Kan?" True asked.

Cerise nodded. "Plenty. Some raiders wouldn't even bother selling us as slaves. They'd rape us then kill us."

True gulped. So they weren't necessarily saved. That was good to know.

"I can't see well with these flashing lights," she told Cerise. "They look big from a distance."

"We should try to get a better look." Cerise waved a hand behind her as she scurried forward, and True followed closely behind.

They flattened themselves behind a loose wall panel as a pair of the attackers appeared at the end of the curved corridor. True squinted to see what she could make out. They were tall and broad, but they didn't seem to be wearing uniforms. She could make out that some of them had shaggy hair and others didn't, but all had a multitude of weapons strapped to their waists.

One of the aliens glanced down, then turned back and shook his head. "Not here. The Raith-Kan may have been telling the truth. They might be dead."

When they'd moved away, True grasped Cerise's arm. "Did you hear that?"

"Who do you think they're talking about?"

"Who cares?" True shook her friend's arm. "They sounded like Drexians."

Cerise tilted her head. "You're right. They were speaking Drexian. Funny, they didn't really look like Drexians."

"They must be," True said, stepping out from their hiding place. "Why else would they speak the language?"

"You don't think they're looking for us, do you?" Now Cerise clutched her arm. "You don't think we're the ones they think are dead?"

True's heart sank. If the Drexians had come looking for her and Cerise and didn't find them, would they leave? If they were convinced the women were dead, they might.

True began running through the ship, hearing the staccato of Cerise's feet behind her. She didn't care anymore if the Raith-Kan found her. She had to locate the Drexian rescue party and tell them that they weren't dead. They were right here.

She rounded a corner and then another, hearing Cerise panting behind her. Where had the Drexians gone? She felt a desperation claw at her throat as she tried to remember the labyrinth they'd gone through to reach their cell and use that memory to find a way out. What if the Drexians left without her, and she never saw Varden again?

No. She squeezed her hands into hard fists. She couldn't let that happen. She turned down another corridor and felt sick. She recognized that door. They'd run right back to where the Raith-Kan had held them.

Resting her hands on her knees, True fought the urge to cry. "I don't know how to get out. I don't know how to find them."

Cerise rested a hand on her back, and the gentle touch almost made her tears fall.

She straightened again, sucking in a breath. Then she heard something that made her stop breathing altogether. Her name. Someone was screaming her name over and over. The noise was muffled, but she could definitely make out her name.

She swung her head toward the door to the cells. It was coming from inside there. Her hand shook as she wrenched open the door, holding it as she took in the sight before her.

A pair of Drexians were holding Varden back as he lunged for a Raith-Kan who lay on the floor, bloody and battered. The captain's face was red and filled with fury as he bellowed her name. She'd never seen him like that. She'd never seen him so out of control, as he struggled to reach the motionless alien. The raw sound of Varden's anguished cries released the dam within her, and the tears flowed freely down her cheeks.

"I'm here," she said, her voice a hoarse croak. No one heard her, so she raised her voice as loud as she could. "I'm right here!"

The Drexians pivoted toward her, their jaws dropping simultaneously. The warriors holding Varden released their grip on him, and he collapsed to the floor, his eyes never leaving her.

"I'm not dead," she told him, smiling through her tears. "I'm right here." She motioned to Cerise. "We're both here."

Varden pushed himself up and staggered toward her, his eyes raking over her body like he couldn't believe what he was seeing. When he reached her, he touched a hand gently to her hair.

"I'm real," she said, laughing. "I promise."

Sweeping her into his arms, Varden crushed his mouth to hers. There was nothing gentle about his possession of her, his mouth devouring hers as he backed her against the wall. She lifted her legs to wrap them around his waist, pulling him closer and moaning as she felt his hardness.

Only when she heard deep chuckling coming from behind them did she realize the other Drexians were still in the room. Not to mention Cerise. Varden must have heard the same low laughter and clearing of throats.

He broke the kiss, breathing heavily and staring down at her with hungry eyes. "I thought I'd lost you. They said they'd put you out the airlock."

She shook her head. "They lied. We got away and were hiding."

He rested his forehead against hers. "I don't want to lose you again. I don't want to be away from you again. Ever."

"Me, either." She ran a hand through his hair.

"I know I don't deserve a mate as young and perfect as you, but I don't care. I can't live without you."

True bit her lower lip. "You're sure I'm not too young and inexperienced for you?"

"Not at all." He kissed her, gently this time. "I think you've proven what a fast learner you are."

Her cheeks heated. "Well, I have a good teacher."

"If you two don't mind," Torven said, working hard to keep a straight face. "I'd really like to get off this horrible ship. I'm afraid I'm going to smell like a Raith-Kan if I don't leave soon, and then my mate won't do any of the things to me that I enjoy so much."

"Ready?" Varden asked her, moving away from the wall.

"To start a life with you?" True kept her legs looped tight around his waist and gave him a seductive smile. "Yes, please."

CHAPTER
TWENTY-NINE

True pressed a panel to the side of the wide window and watched the metallic shade rise slowly, revealing a dusky brown landscape dotted with brambly bushes and low gray buildings, with an outcropping of tall rocks in the distance. The outpost on Graxos—and the temporary housing for residents of the Boat—may not have been glamorous or scenic, but she'd never been happier to be anywhere in her life.

She spotted some big Drexians striding from building to building in their uniforms, looking purposeful and busy. Even though the Boat was undergoing repairs, it would still be some time until they could all return safely. Not that True minded.

She stretched and yawned. She was still recovering from her entire abduction and escape ordeal, so she'd been sleeping late every day since they'd arrived. That meant she was waking up alone, since Varden was up early to meet with his officers, but she didn't mind that, either. Especially since he usually popped back in to visit her in the middle of the day, and she was able to distract him for at least an hour before he had to put his uniform back on and return to duty.

True smiled to herself. She loved messing up his buttoned-up appearance. And she especially loved how his formal persona fell away when they were in bed, although he liked to give orders. Orders she didn't mind obeying. She did miss having him naked and wet under the waterfall, though. The cramped shower here did not even come close to replicating the experience, not that they hadn't tried.

Crossing to the built-in dresser that held their clothes—or at least the clothes that had been provided for her when she arrived—she slid open the door and ran a finger across his neatly hung uniforms. He didn't own much else in the way of clothing except for a Kranji uniform and a couple of casual shirts.

Varden didn't bother with PJs, and True didn't mind one bit that he slept in the nude. She loved being able to roll over and run her hands down his bare chest or bare ass. Of course, that usually led to her nightgown ending up in a heap on the floor, which she didn't mind, either.

She hummed as she pulled one of his uniform shirts off the hanger and slipped out of her nightgown, then she put on the dark military shirt and buttoned it up. Lifting the collar to her nose, she inhaled the scent of him and felt a rush of heat between her legs.

"Now that's what I like to see."

His deep voice made her spin around, and she saw him standing inside the door. "I didn't hear you come in."

"You looked preoccupied." He walked toward her slowly, never taking his eyes off hers. "I liked watching."

Her cheeks warmed as he reached her. "What else do you like to watch?"

A low growl rumbled in his throat. "You on my cock."

Her breath hitched in her throat, and her pulse fluttered as he traced one finger down her throat, skimming over the fabric of his stiff shirt until he reached her breast. Without dropping his gaze, he rolled her nipple between his thumb and finger, and it hardened in response.

True bit her lower lip, heat coiling in her belly and making it do nervous flips. The Drexian had barely touched her, and she already felt the slickness between her thighs.

She raised her hands to the shirt's top button. "You want me to take it off?"

"Not yet." He pulled off his own captain's uniform, tossing both the pants and shirt onto the bed and peeling off his tight black underwear. When he was naked, he sat down on one of the scoop-back chairs. "First, I want you to ride."

His forceful voice sent a thrill through her. Even so, True swallowed hard as she eyed the huge cock jutting up thick from his body. She might not be a virgin anymore, but his size made her body stretch to take him each time.

She straddled him, tucking her knees up beside his legs and notching his cock at her opening.

"Arms up," he ordered, pulling her hands and positioning them over her head. He then clamped his hands on her hips and moved her so that she took the crown of his cock, the hard flesh parting her.

True inhaled sharply, her body jerking instinctively. He held her in place, his gaze molten as it locked on hers. "This is mine." He moved her down onto his shaft. "All of this hot tightness is mine. No one else's. Ever."

She moaned and tried to gyrate her hips as his rigid length stretched her. The mixture of pleasure and pain made her want to beg him to stop and beg him for more. With one final, hard thrust, his cock filled her completely.

She gasped, the air leaving her in a rush.

"Say it." Varden's voice was dark and dominant. "Say that you're mine."

Desire made her almost lightheaded. "I'm yours, Varden. Only yours."

His fingers biting into the flesh on her hips, he stroked her up and down. "Gods, you're so tight and so wet for me, cinnara."

She couldn't speak as he pumped her on his cock, the feeling of being filled by him making her cry out with each deep thrust.

"Take it off," he ordered, not slowing his pace.

She blinked at him before realizing he meant his military shirt that she wore. It took all her concentration to unbutton the shirt and shrug it off her shoulders. He groaned when she was completely bare, her breasts bouncing as she rode him.

True dragged both of her hands down his chest and the bumpy ridges of his stomach muscles, then she arched back and braced her palms on his thick legs.

His eyes closed for a moment as he moaned. "Gods, True."

"Now you watch," she said. "Watch how you split me."

His gaze was white-hot as he watched the place where their bodies joined, and the muscles in his neck strained. "You're stretched so tight around my cock."

"Mmhmm." She leaned back, opening her legs wider.

"You like taking me deep, don't you, True?" he asked, finding her clit with one thumb and circling it.

Heat stormed through her, his words and his urgent touch making her teeter on the edge. "Yes, Varden. I love you fucking me hard."

He dipped his thumb between her slick folds, then returned it to her swollen nub and swirled his thumb faster.

Her body splintered apart, contracting around him as she screamed and convulsed, one hand falling forward to brace on his chest. Before she could catch her breath, he stood and strode over to the bed, flipping her so that she was on all fours, and he stood behind her. He spread her legs wider and tilted her ass up before dragging his cock through her wet folds and then powering into her.

True grasped the sheets as he pistoned into her, lowering her head and feeling his cock go deeper. A few more hard thrusts, and he roared as his own release overpowered him, and he surged hot inside her.

Her legs trembled as she collapsed onto the bed, feeling his warm body cover hers, his ragged breath warm on her neck. He swept her hair out of the way and kissed her gently, his soft lips sending tremors down her spine. "Have I mentioned lately how much I love you?"

She laughed. "A few times last night, I think. After I sucked your cock."

He wrapped an arm underneath her and cupped one breast. "I do love the way you suck my cock." His voice became husky. "I love everything about you, cinnara."

She twisted her head to face him. "And I love you."

"You sure you don't regret your choice?" He stroked a finger down her cheek.

"Not for a second, Captain." She made a humming noise in the back of her throat as she felt his cock still hard inside her and her muscles twitching around it. "I'll gladly take your orders for the rest of my life, as long as you keep *that* up."

He shifted thickly between her legs. "Your wish is my command."

CHAPTER
THIRTY

A beep at the door made her stomach somersault. He'd only left a few minutes ago. Was he back again so soon? Not that she wouldn't mind going another round.

"Come on in, Captain. You know it's open," she called, stretching out on the bed in an alluring pose.

The tapping footsteps that entered did not sound like Varden.

"Goodness," Cerise said when she saw True's pose. "I thought we were just friends, sweetie."

True sat up quickly, her cheeks warm, as she pulled the sheet around her. "I thought you were..."

"Oh, I know who you thought I was." Cerise touched a hand to her repaired wig. "It's no secret anymore."

True couldn't help grinning as she hurried to the dresser and pulled out a pair of black drawstring pants and a soft T-shirt. She was glad it wasn't a secret. She knew Varden had had to do some serious explaining to High Command as to why he was requesting a human mate, and one who'd originally rejected the idea of being a tribute bride. They'd even asked her to appear before them to assure their members that she wanted to be matched with the older Drexian.

She thought back to Varden flushing with pride as she'd announced in no uncertain terms to the elder Drexians that he was the only Drexian she wanted, and that she was head-over-heels in love with him. After much muttering and many disapproving looks, they'd finally given their approval. She'd worried that Varden would be punished in some way, but his valor on the primitive planet and his determination to save her and Cerise from the Raith-Kan had been noted, so he'd retained his command.

"Any chance you'll be joining the brides today?" Cerise asked, her back turned while True dressed. "You know, you are one of them now."

"You can turn around," she said to the alien. "I may have agreed to marry Varden, but that doesn't mean I'm a tribute bride. Plus, Serge and Reina are still unaccounted for. I can't plan my wedding without them."

Cerise's smile fell from her face. "They still haven't tracked down where their shuttle might have gone. It's the only one still missing."

True regretted bringing up the subject, as she knew how close the Perogling had grown to Serge and Reina, since she'd been helping them with wedding planning. "I'm sure the Drexians will track them down. They found us, didn't they?"

Cerise walked to a low chair and sank into it. "What if they ended up somewhere less hospitable than the planet we crashed onto? They might not have gotten as lucky with the natives as we did." Her eyes pinched together, forming a crease between her arched brows. "What if *they* were captured by slavers?"

True's stomach knotted as she thought back to their time in the dank, cold cell on the Raith-Kan ship. She didn't know Serge and Reina well—and hadn't laid eyes on the new group of tribute brides—but the thought of them being held captive made her feel ill. "We have to think positive. They've sent some of the best Inferno Force trackers after them."

Cerise nodded absently. "You're right. Of course you're right. You know Kos went, too?"

"Kos? Varden's first officer?" She hadn't known.

"One of the missing tribute brides was his."

True put a hand on her belly as it churned, and she walked over to the small food prep area tucked into one corner of the suite. "I had no idea. Varden didn't mention it."

"Have you paused to talk since you've been back?" Cerise asked with an arch smile.

True tried to shoot her a severe look but couldn't pull it off. Not without puking, at least. The thought of Kos searching for his missing bride made a wave of nausea rise up in her throat. She leaned on the counter and focused on breathing deeply.

Since Varden was the captain of the Boat, they'd gotten one of the chief officers' suites on the outpost. Even though True didn't like to think of using her new mate's rank for perks, she did like having drinks and food on hand. Especially since thinking about the missing women kept making her feel sick. And the news about Kos and his missing tribute didn't help. She felt a certain fondness for Varden's first officer after what they'd all been through together.

Her hands shook as she filled a glass from the spout in the wall, touching the button to activate the flow of the fizzy beverage. "Can I get you something to drink?"

Before Cerise could answer, the door beeped. The Perogling jumped up and crossed to it. "You expecting more visitors?"

True took a sip of the cold drink, her gut unclenching, as she shook her head.

"Oh, good," Ella said when the door opened to reveal her. "Two for the price of one."

She strode into the room, holding a tablet in one hand. Her dark curls were piled on top of her head, and she wore her usual snug black pants and tucked-in white button-down shirt. "I need your opinion on something I'm working on for the refurbishment of the Boat."

True grinned. One of the things she loved most about her best friend was that the woman always had a project. Never one to sit still, she had to be doing something, and usually the things she did were pretty cool. Ella had worked with the Boat's wedding decor designer to create spectacular holographic details for the weddings, then she'd assisted the Drexians in tracking down a kidnapped and brainwashed warrior, and now True had no doubt she was in the thick of the work being done to get the Boat back into shape after the Kronock attack.

"You know I always like to help you with your work," True said, taking a chair across from Ella as the woman sat down and put her tablet on the low, clear table between them.

Ella gave her a quick, bright smile. "You know how we had a holographic Christmas tree for the party?" She didn't wait for a response. "Well, after doing that, I realized we probably aren't taking advantage of the holographic tech throughout the station. I mean, I know it's used in the fantasy suites and the holodecks, but what if we could use holo-emitters to create fantasy settings all over the station?"

True swirled a section of hair around her finger. "Sounds complicated. Didn't creating the Christmas tree stress you out?"

Ella waved her hand. "That was because I had to coordinate the snowfall to start after the fireworks that shot out of the top of the tree. I'm not talking about anything so synchronized on a day-to-day basis."

Cerise perched on the arm of True's chair. "So what *are* you talking?"

"Seasons," Ella said, with a small sigh. "I don't know about you, but the Boat can be too perfect. I miss seasons. I thought I could set a program to make the promenade have seasons—and weather."

Cerise cocked her head to one side. "I hope you aren't talking about Perogling seasons. On my home world, we have an entire season where the ground bubbles up black goo and you have to wear boots up to your hips."

Ella wrinkled her nose. "No black goo season."

True stifled a giggle behind her glass. "I lived in Alabama, remember. We didn't have many seasons, although mosquito season seemed to last longer and longer each year."

"No mosquito season, either," Ella said. "But I thought we could at least have sweater weather in the fall and snowfall for winter, then have lots of flowers bloom in spring."

"That might be nice," True said.

Ella looked up at both woman and then flopped back in her chair. "I know it's silly, but I just need something to keep my mind busy."

Another sound at the door made Cerise leap to her feet and bustle over, opening the door and beaming when she saw more women on the other side.

"So this is where the party is," Shreya said as she and Katie came into the room, followed by a pregnant Mandy, who waddled slightly as she walked. "Mind if we join you?" She glanced at Ella. "Dakar said you might be here."

"Come on in." True stood. "But I don't think I have enough chairs."

Katie flipped her curling strawberry-blond hair off her shoulder. "Don't sweat it. We just needed to get out of our own rooms. The quarters here are a lot smaller than on the Boat." She glanced around. "Except for this room. This isn't half bad."

Shreya winked at True. "I guess it pays to be seduced by the captain of the Boat, eh, mate?"

True's face heated, even though she knew Shreya was only teasing her. "Who says I didn't seduce him?"

Katie let out a loud laugh. "We can always ask Cerise. She was there."

"As long as the story isn't too hot," Mandy said. "I'd hate to go into early labor."

Cerise giggled and shook her head. "One thing I learned very well working in pleasure houses—never reveal a lady's secrets."

True motioned for Mandy to take her seat. "Here, you should sit."

"Normally, I'd say no, but the baby seems to have settled low, and it's killing my back." She lowered herself gingerly into the chair. "Drexian babies are bigger than human babies—and more active. Did you know that?" She let out a high-pitched laugh. "Me either. I mean, it makes sense. Drexians are huge and aren't known for sitting around, but this baby never stops moving."

Katie positioned herself behind Mandy and rubbed her shoulders. "What you need to do is relax."

"Relax?" Mandy put a hand to her forehead. "How can I relax when Serge and Reina—not to mention a new group of tribute brides—are missing?"

"Come on, Mandy," Katie said. "You work in the medical bay. You know it isn't good for you or the baby to be so stressed out."

Mandy let out a long breath. "I know, I know."

"The Drexian search party will find them," True said, repeating what she'd told Cerise. "They're the best. They found Cerise and me. They'll find Serge and Reina and the brides."

"She's right, Mandy," Ella said. "We found Shreya when she was taken by Vox."

"Exactly," Shreya said. "It's only a matter of time before they're back here, and Serge is driving everyone crazy."

True chugged the rest of her sparkling water, rubbing her belly as it settled. "I hope he doesn't want to start planning my wedding right away."

Ella's expression brightened. "I've been so caught up with the evacuation and settling into the colony that I've completely neglected your wedding." She picked up her tablet and began tapping. "Have you thought about what kind of ceremony you and Varden want?"

Another wave of nausea made True press her fingers to her lips. She shook her head.

"She was a virgin up until about a week ago," Cerise said. "Give her a little time to adjust."

Mandy eyed True. "I'd say she has just under ten months to adjust."

"What?" Ella looked up. "They won't want to wait ten months to get married."

"I'm not talking about their wedding," Mandy said, a smug expression on her face. "I'm talking about when their baby will be born."

True's mouth fell open, and she almost dropped her glass. "Baby? I can't be...?"

Mandy leaned forward. "Let me guess. You've felt queasy. You've been sleeping a lot." She pointed at True's chest. "And your boobs are bigger."

Ella gaped at Mandy, who just shrugged. "What? I notice these things."

All the women turned their attention to True as she slowly nodded. "I thought I was just recovering, but maybe..."

Cerise threw her small arms around the woman. "This is so exciting. Another baby! And it's the captain's!"

Ella dabbed at her eyes, beaming at True. "I'll bet he never expected to be a father."

A tingling warmth spread throughout her body as she envisioned Varden's face when she told him. "He's getting a lot he never expected."

TRUE FELT the energy in the room shift before she even heard Varden walk inside. She turned from where she was refilling her glass, and held her breath as she watched him walk into the room and take in the group of women that had gathered.

"Hey, Captain," Mandy said, standing up with one hand on her belly and one on the armrest of the chair for support. "We were just leaving."

"We were?" Cerise asked, as Shreya tugged on her arm.

Mandy shot the Perogling a pointed look. "Yes, we were. We've got that thing, remember?"

"I remember the thing," Bridget said, winking at True and putting an arm around Mandy.

Ella rolled her eyes, leaning in to True and giving her a quick squeeze. "Sorry our crew has the subtlety of a sledgehammer."

True smiled, releasing her breath as the women exited the room in a flurry of chatter and laughter. She took a swig of her fizzy water and felt the coolness settle her stomach. She wasn't sure if this was nerves or morning sickness, but whichever it was, she knew she'd feel better once she told him.

True honestly wasn't sure how her mate would react. He'd never given a moment's thought to being a father. Not in years, at least.

And they hadn't been together for long, although they'd certainly made the most of the time they'd had. Come to think of it, she shouldn't have been at all surprised. They hadn't been able to keep their hands off each other since the first time he'd claimed her at the waterfall.

She touched a hand to her belly, which betrayed no clue of the change going on inside her.

"What was that all about?" Varden asked, unfastening his uniform jacket and tossing it over the nearest chair.

The tight T-shirt underneath showed off his muscular chest, and True felt a rush of heat between her legs. She shook her head and reminded herself to focus on what she needed to do.

"We were just catching up," she said. "Mandy was talking about getting ready for the baby."

Varden chuckled. "Dorn is as jumpy as a Braxtian hopping beetle. It's nice to see that the Inferno Force warriors can be terrified by something."

"Would you be?" True asked, trying to make her tone casual.

"Would I be what?"

"Nervous about a baby?"

He laughed again. "That's something I've never had to think about, why do...?" The words died out in his throat as he stared at her. "Is that your way of telling me...?" Tears filled his eyes. "Are we...?"

She nodded, his form blurry through her own tears. "I'm pretty sure. I've been feeling queasy for about a week and apparently Mandy noticed that my boobs are—"

She squealed as he crossed the room in a couple of long strides and swept her up into his arms, cutting off the rest of her explanation with a deep kiss that she felt all the way to her toes. When he pulled away, she felt breathless. And happy. Happier than she'd ever been.

"We're going to have a baby?" His voice was thick with emotion. "I'm going to be a father?" He took a deep breath, and a smile lit up his face. "I'm going to be a father."

Tears threatened the backs of her eyes again. "You're going to be amazing."

"I thought I was happy before, but now..."

"I know," she said. "I feel the same way. Life with you couldn't get any better and then it did."

He stroked a hand down the side of her face, then put her down quickly and glanced at her stomach. "I didn't hold you too tight, did I? Are you feeling sick now?"

"No." She giggled at the nervous way he held her. "And just because I'm carrying your baby doesn't mean I'm made of glass." She gave him a shy smile. "We can still do everything we normally do."

He placed a protective hand over her flat belly. "Everything?"

She took his hand and pulled his toward the bed. "Why don't I show you?"

EPILOGUE

Hope pushed her long blond hair off her face and blinked up at the bright lights. The ceiling was low and gleamed silver and didn't do anything to help her aching eyes.

"I'm so relieved you're awake, sweetie."

She rotated her head slowly and saw the towering creature standing next to her, wringing her spindly hands. She recognized this woman. She'd met her along with a very short, strange man when they'd both tried to convince her that she was on an alien space station. She almost laughed at the concept all over again.

She'd heard some crazy things in her life—her mother had run her own ashram before running off with a traveling shaman, so woo-woo things weren't something new—but not even her crazy mother would have believed in alien abduction. Hope peered up at the woman's pale gray skin and swish of blue hair. Not that this Reina creature wasn't doing a good job of selling it. She looked seriously otherworldly.

"You aren't hurt, are you?" Reina asked, her high voice anxious.

Hope pushed herself up on her elbows and realized she was lying flat on a long bench. "Hurt? No." She glanced around. "What happened to the Caribbean bungalow?"

"Your fantasy suite?" Reina nibbled the corner of her lip. "I hope it's fine. We won't know until we return to the Boat. *If* we ever return to the Boat."

"The Boat? Oh, right. That's what you called the alien space station, right? The place you claim we're on."

"Oh, we're not on the Boat now."

Hope swiveled her head. She could believe that. The room they were currently in looked nothing like the luxurious suite that overlooked the blue Caribbean waters she'd been in earlier. It was all steel, with curved walls and no detachable furniture. Only long benches attached to the walls and a nearly circular door with what looked like a porthole in the center. "So now we're not on an alien space station?"

Reina gave her a concerned look. "Don't you remember leaving the station and getting on the escape shuttle?"

Hope touched her head. Now that the woman mentioned it, she did have hazy memories of running onto a plane of some kind with Reina and the short man with purple hair and a few other women who'd looked just as confused as her. "I guess."

"You were knocked out when our ship was taken captive, so I'm not surprised you don't remember everything."

"Captive?" Hope stood and turned, her mouth dropping open. Behind her was a half-moon-shaped window with a view of an inky-black sky dotted with hundreds of twinkling stars. "Where are we?"

Reina worked her hands together, her voice little more than a breathy whisper. "I'm afraid we're on one of the Ganthar pirate ships."

Hope's stomach dropped. She didn't know what that meant, but she had a very bad feeling about it.

THANK YOU FOR READING CRAVED!

If you liked this alien abduction romance, you'll love STOLEN. When Hope is taken by space pirates, her Drexian fiancé Kos will do whatever it takes to find her. And though she's determined to return to her own planet, he's already decided that she's his fated mate... One-click STOLEN Now>

"I literally couldn't put the book down. I definitely didn't see the outcome coming and Tana Stone had me at the edge of my seat!!"- Amazon Reviewer

This book has been edited and proofed, but typos are like little gremlins that like to sneak in when we're not looking. If you spot a typo, please report it to: tana@tanastone.com
Thank you!!

PREVIEW OF STOLEN—TRIBUTE BRIDES OF THE DREXIAN WARRIORS #9

Chapter One

Kos rocked back on his heels, dragging a hand through his short, brown hair, as he peered out the window of the ship. Slashes of light zoomed by as they cut through the blackness of space, the spaceship flying at warp speed toward their destination.

Even though the computerized beeps and whirring sounds reminded him of the bridge on the space station—casually referred to as the Boat— the Inferno Force ship was worlds away from it. Not that he minded. He found the dimly lit ship with its stripped-down, steel interior to be a welcome change from the brightness of the station. This ship was a bit battered, and more than a little bare-bones, but it flew fast and had impressive firepower. Both things he was grateful for on the rescue mission.

As a Drexian, he was part of the warrior species known throughout the galaxy as fierce fighters who defended others. Drexians had saved countless worlds from destruction from the violent Kronock. The also defended Earth—unbeknownst to most of the planet's inhabitants—from alien invasion. In return, Earth provided the Drexians, who hadn't produced females in a generation, with brides for their warriors. Tribute brides, they were called. It was one of these Earth brides that Kos was on a mission to rescue. *His* tribute bride.

Not that he'd ever laid eyes on her. He bit his lower lip as he thought about putting off meeting the human when they'd been on the Boat. He'd been an idiot, and now he was paying the price. Of course, he'd never anticipated that she would be kidnapped along with the other new brides or that he would crash land on an alien planet as the station evacuated. Still, he'd wasted his chance and now she was missing. He grunted and slammed a palm against the glass.

One of the Inferno Force warriors spun around and eyed him. "Don't worry. We'll get your tribute back for you."

Kos nodded—remembering that the pilot's name was Kalex—but didn't respond as the soldier with shaggy brown hair and tattoos banding his arms turned back around.

He knew he was lucky to be with the team of Inferno Force warriors sent to locate and rescue the abducted tribute brides and their handlers, but he also knew he didn't belong with the edgy fighters. Where he followed protocol, they broke the rules. He prided himself on regulation-short hair and a pristine uniform. Inferno Force warriors let their hair grow long and sported tight shirts that showed off plenty of ink. Still, he knew he should be grateful to be on the mission with them.

The rough Drexian warriors rarely let others join them on missions. They preferred to operate on the outskirts of the galaxy, out of reach of the Drexian High Command. Commanders and captains of Inferno Force ran their fleets and ships with a fight hard, play hard mentality. It was a sharp contrast to the protocol expected from officers on the Boat, but one Kos was glad to adapt to since he'd had to fight for the right to join them.

Kos thought back to the meeting where the rescue mission had been finalized and to his own out-of-character behavior. He'd finally been allowed only because one of the missing human women was the tribute bride assigned to him, and he'd argued vehemently that he be allowed to join the hunt for her. His face warmed as he remembered brandishing a blade and threatening harm to anyone who tried to keep him off the mission. The Inferno Force captain leading the mission had liked his insubordination. Any warrior with that much passion was welcome on his crew, he'd said once Kos had stopped yelling. Kos did feel passionate about finding his tribute bride. Even though he'd never met her. Especially because he'd never met her.

While he'd been stuck on the station's bridge during the Kronock attack, his tribute bride, Hope, had been meeting with her wedding planner and liaison and learning all about the Drexians and the secret treaty with Earth and how the Boat had been designed specifically to help Drexian warriors woo their new brides and to assist the humans in planning their dream weddings. He'd missed his introduction to her when the station had begun evacuation procedures, and he'd been further delayed when the shuttle he'd been on had crashed onto a jungle planet along with Captain Varden, one of the reject tributes, and the Perogling.

His only comfort had been knowing that his intended bride had been safely evacuated by her wedding planner and liaison, along with a few other human tributes. He knew enough about the Gatazoid wedding planner, Serge, and the Vexling liaison, Reina, to know that they would take good care of the tributes. Of course, that was before he'd discovered that the shuttled with the handlers and tributes had disappeared en route to the Drexian rendezvous outpost where all the residents of the Boat had gone during the Kronock attack.

You should have been with her, he told himself for the hundredth time. His stomach had been a hard ball of fear and regret since he'd found out that Hope was missing. Even though he'd never met the female, he knew she'd been his to protect, and he'd failed.

Just like you failed before, a little voice in the back of his head whispered. He shook it off, but the cold ball in his gut tightened. He would not fail this time. No matter what.

"Approaching the last known coordinates of the shuttle," Kalex said, tapping his fingers to slow their speed.

The ship came out of warp and the streaks of light became pinpoints again, flickering in the inky space around them.

Kos stepped forward, scanning the emptiness. "They're gone now. Any residual power signatures we can track?"

More tapping on the console. "Nothing from our shuttle, but then again, we do have the most sophisticated shielding technology in the galaxy. There is a faint trace of something, but..."

"Why are we slowing?" Brok, the Inferno Force captain leading the mission, strode onto the bridge, his heavy boots announcing his arrival along with his loud voice. Like all Drexians, he was big and bulky, but he seemed to be more tattooed and more scarred than most. Even for an Inferno Force warrior. He wore his dark hair long with a braid down one side, although there was nothing remotely feminine about it. A scar slashed through one eyebrow, but that only served to draw more attention to his aquamarine blue eyes.

"We've reached the last know location of the vessel," his pilot said without turning.

Brok grunted, nodding at Kos, his mouth quirking up slightly. "Glad to see you lost the uniform jacket, officer."

Kos shifted. "Yes, sir."

He'd taken off his Drexian military jacket after he'd realized that no one on the Inferno Force crew wore them—and after the captain had told him to. Even though it felt odd to be in only a black T-shirt and pants on the bridge of a ship, he had to admit it was more comfortable.

"Anything out there?" Brok asked, turning his attention back to his pilot.

"I was just telling Kos that I'm picking up on something," Kalex said, his fingers flying across the shiny, black console. "It's a power signature we haven't seen in a long time."

Brok folded his arms over his chest. "Tell me that's a good thing."

Kalex spun around. "Only if you think Ganthar pirates are good."

"Grek." The captain spat out the word, his face darkening.

"Ganthar pirates?" Kos asked, looking from the pilot to the captain. "I thought they'd all but disappeared in our sector."

"Apparently not," Kalex muttered as he turned back to his console.

Kos drew in a breath, trying not to think about what this might mean for Hope and all the abducted females. "Okay, so we go after these pirates."

"I can track their signature," Kalex said. "I don't know how much of a lead they have on us, but we'll hunt them down."

Brok nodded. "Send a transmission to our sister ship. We'll need them to rendezvous. Ganthar pirates aren't something we mess around with."

"They can't be any match for Drexian technology or Inferno Force," Kos said.

"They aren't," the captain said, "but they also aren't constrained by honor or fair fighting. We've been ambushed by Ganthar pirates before. They aren't to be trusted."

Kos swallowed hard. His bride was potentially being held by pirates with no honor. Even though he didn't know her, he felt sick at the thought of one of the small, feminine humans being held at the mercy of space pirates. He'd seen images of Hope—her long blonde hair, her warm brown eyes. His chest swelled at the thought of holding her in his arms and telling her how sorry he was.

Sorry for not meeting her earlier. Sorry for not being with her during the evacuation. Sorry for not preventing her ship from being intercepted.

Brok clapped a thick hand on Kos's shoulder. "We will get her back. We will get all of them back."

Kos nodded. Inferno Force never doubted their abilities. He knew that came from years of fighting off the Kronock. Even though their enemy had recently revealed previously unknown technology, and had landed a few considerable blows to Drexian forces, Inferno Force was no less sure in that they would beat them back.

Kos wished he had the same confidence of these warriors. His success had always come from working harder than everyone else, nothing else. He'd become the first officer of the Boat by putting in long hours, not by just knowing he could do it. That kind of confidence seemed to be relegated to warriors like those on Inferno Force.

But he had become first officer, he reminded himself. The officer that Captain Varden trusted above all others. The officer who would put the job above everything else and never let his superiors down.

Which is why you didn't meet your bride, the nagging voice said. You were too busy on the bridge. She was evacuated without you while you got Captain Varden off.

Kos squeezed his hands into fists. He had never imagined she would be taken. How could he have? It was unthinkable.

"Setting a new course," Kalex said, moments before the ship jumped to warp speed again.

"Ready to battle some pirates?" Brok asked him.

Kos squared his shoulders and met the captain's gaze. "Ready, sir."

"Good." Brok propelled him off the bridge. "Now let's go make you look like you're ready."

Chapter Two

Hope paced a tight circle in her cell, spinning on her heel each time she reached the long bench that ran along the back wall. She'd coiled her long blonde hair up into a topknot, but it kept coming loose and falling back down.

"You really should try to relax, hon," the blue-haired woman named Reina said from where she sat on the bench, her long legs crossed at the knees and her top leg jiggling up and down.

Holly paused to take in the alien for a moment, wondering how the creature could sound so calm when she was clearly just as nervous as she was. "How am I supposed to relax? I was abducted from Earth and taken to a space station where I was told I'd been picked to be a tribute bride for a Drexian warrior—whatever that is —and before I could even absorb all that ridiculousness, we were evacuating the supposed space station because we were being attacked by other aliens and then our ship was intercepted and I was knocked unconscious. When I finally woke up, you tell me that we've been taken captive by Ganthar pirates. That was a few days ago, and we're still stuck in this cell with no idea where we're going or what's going to happen to us. Did I leave anything out?"

Reina gave a nervous laugh. "No. I think that about covers it, but you forgot that the Drexians will be coming after us."

"Right." Hope snapped her fingers. "The mythical Drexian warriors who are, according to you, the biggest badasses in the galaxy."

"They are," Reina said, her gray face earnest as she bobbed her head up and down. "And I have no doubt they're searching for us right now. I'm sure your groom is sick with worry."

Hope put her hands on her hips. "My groom? That's a phrase I never thought I'd use. If there's a Drexian warrior that I'm matched with—or so you claim—then why didn't I meet him earlier? Was he not on the space station?"

Reina nibbled her lower lip. "Actually, he was, but..."

"But he was as wild about the idea of marrying a stranger as I was?" Hope resumed her pacing and whipped her hair up into a knot again.

"Oh, no. That's not it. I'm sure he was very pleased to be

matched with you," Reina said. "But Kos is the first officer of the space station, so I'm sure he was incredibly busy when we had to evacuate. It had nothing to do with you."

Hope raised an eyebrow. "Nothing to do with me? How flattering."

Reina smiled. "I'm glad you think so."

So much for aliens getting sarcasm, Hope thought. It hadn't been bad being stuck in the cell with the tall alien who claimed to be a Vexling. At least she'd had someone to talk to, but the nervous creature definitely didn't get her sense of humor.

"So, we just have to hope that these Drexians get here before what...? The pirates make us walk the space plank?"

Reina's gray skin lost a few shades. "Oh, no. I don't think they would do that." She tapped a bony finger on the side of her face. "I don't even think they have a space plank."

"Kidding," Hope muttered. "What do these Ganthar pirates do when they take prisoners anyway?"

Reina stood and crossed to the circular door with a small round window, peering out into the dim, gunmetal gray corridor. "I don't know for sure. Usually they steal things they can sell."

Hope gulped. "We're going to be sold? Like as slaves?"

Reina shook her head. "I'm sure we'll be rescued by the Drexians before that happens."

Hope sank onto the metal bench and put her head in her hands. Even though she'd pitched a fit when she'd woken up on the Drexian space station, she wished she was there now. The holographic fantasy suite that had been designed to look, smell, and feel like a Caribbean bungalow seemed like a lifetime away now. Why had she been such a pain in the ass to everyone when she'd found herself overlooking the crystal blue waters? Why had she been horrible to the little wedding planner with purple hair?

Because they'd freaked her out, that was why. You couldn't expect to tell someone they'd been taken off their planet by aliens and conscripted to be a bride and have them go along with it. Her reaction—disbelief followed by hostility and threats followed by hysteria—had been totally normal. At least for her.

Hope had been on her own for so long that the idea of being told what to do by anyone made her bristle. And the idea of her entire future being dictated to her made Hope want to run away screaming. She'd always prided herself on her independence—it's what came from having a space cadet mother who'd eventually run off with her shaman—and no way was she going to be mated to some alien stranger without a fight.

"What happens then?" She looked up at Reina. "What happens when we're rescued?"

Reina's expression brightened. "Then we go back to the Boat, or if the station was damaged too much, to the rendezvous outpost."

"So, no chance I'll be taken back to Earth?"

"Once a human is taken to be a tribute bride, they can't be returned to Earth," Reina said. "Can you imagine the hysteria if women went back and started talking about aliens and space stations and invasions?"

The woman had a point. It would create pandemonium.

"What if I promised not to talk?"

Reina smiled at her. "Of course, I would believe you, hon, but it's not up to me. I'm just a liaison. I don't make the rules."

Hope nodded. It probably didn't make sense to worry about the Drexians taking her back to Earth when she hadn't even been rescued yet. Reina seemed convinced it was inevitable, but they'd already been captive for several days. Hope didn't want to think about the other alternative—being sold into alien slavery. Being a tribute bride didn't sound so bad in comparison.

Reina walked over and set next to her on the bench. "Just you wait until you meet some of the other brides. You'll love them. There are women from all over. Even a couple from New Zeenland, like you."

"New Zealand," Hope corrected. "There are really other Kiwis on the station?"

Reina nodded. "Not a lot, but there are some. Tribute brides come from all over. I know you'll make some good friends once you get to know them."

Hope returned Reina's eager smile. She wasn't so sure about that. Making friends had never been one of her strengths. It was why she'd spent the past few years traveling around the world as a travel blogger. She preferred to be on the move, meeting new people all the time, but never stopping to get too attached to anyone.

It was the same philosophy she had for men. Meet a bunch, have fun, move on. No one got attached. No one got hurt.

"Maybe," she said, trying not to make any promises she couldn't keep.

Reina patted her hand, opening her mouth to say something as the door to their cell opened.

Both women jumped to their feet. No one had come in since they'd been pushed inside days ago. Meals had been passed through a slat at the bottom of the door and no one had responded to her pounding.

The tall alien who stepped inside carried a large weapon of some kind, his eyes raking over both of them. They settled on Reina. "You're a Vexling?"

Reina worked her hands together, letting out a small squeak in response.

The alien pirate jerked his head. "Come with me."

Reina looked at Hope. "I can't leave my tribute. You see, I'm a liaison for the tribute brides and I can't leave her alone— "

"Now!" The yell made both Hope and Reina jump as he lifted the hefty weapon onto his shoulder and aimed it at Hope. "Unless you want me to eliminate your reason for staying behind."

Hope grabbed for Reina hand and squeezed it. "It's okay. I'll be fine." She didn't believe a word she was saying, but she needed the Vexling to go without either of them getting hurt.

Reina's lips became a thin white line, but she nodded. "Don't worry. I'm sure they just want to talk to me. I'll be back before you know it." She squeezed Hope's hand back. "Serge is in the cell next to us, and the other brides are across the corridor, so you're not totally alone."

The alien pirate snorted a laugh. "You mean the Gatazoid? We sold him yesterday. His kind fetch a high price on the market."

Reina's hands went limp in hers. "You sold Serge?"

The pirate's lips curled into a sneer. "And the other females. No one had seen humans before, but apparently the small creatures appeal to some." The way he looked at Hope, she knew he did not count himself in that group, which was fine by her. "You're the last one to go, Vexling."

"Go?" Reina's voice was barely audible. "You're selling me?"

"That's right. We've got a buyer looking for a Vexling." He shrugged. "Something about protocol."

Hope instinctively tightened her grip on Reina's hand. "You can't just sell people like this."

He laughed and his belly shook. "Beg your pardon, girlie, but we can. Don't worry, though. We're not selling you." He looked her up and down. "The captain likes the look of you."

Hope's mouth went dry. That didn't sound good.

"Move it, Vexling," the pirate yelled again. "Before I have to come in and drag you out."

Hope released Reina's hand and gave her a little push, even though what she really wanted to do was jump in front of her to keep her from leaving. "Don't worry. I'll be fine."

Reina's wide eyes glistened with tears, and Hope forced a fake smile onto her face.

"The Drexians are coming for me, right?" she whispered. "Well, when they do, I promise to come find you and get you back."

Reina stumbled forward and let herself be taken out of the cell, her gaze never leaving Hope's face. When the door slammed shut, Hope collapsed onto the bench, trying to steady her ragged breath and keep herself from crying.

She may not have known Reina well or for long, but the blue-haired woman had been kind to her. And they been in the mess together.

Now she was alone. Again.

To be continued...

To order STOLEN, click HERE!

PREVIEW OF BOUNTY— BARBARIANS OF THE SAND PLANET #1

A NEW SERIES BY TANA STONE!

CHAPTER ONE

"Are they shooting at us?" Danica asked, grabbing the edge of a smooth metal console as she stepped onto the bridge and the ship heaved to one side. She tasted blood as she bit the inside of her mouth and flinched from the pain. *Son of a bitch.*

She and Bexli had just brought their latest captive onboard, and she'd given the order to take off, hoping the rival bounty hunters who'd also been in pursuit hadn't seen them. From the staccato sounds of gunfire, she guessed that her plan of slipping out unnoticed was shot to hell.

She took in the familiar sight of the compact bridge--a round flat panel console in the center of the room with view screens suspended above it, smaller individual consoles forming a half moon around the main one, and a final ring of screened consoles against the circular walls. A long narrow slit of a window gave them a view out the front of the ship, but had a steel shade they could lower for security. Nearly every part of the room was composed of metal that was long past gleaming and looked nearly black with age and grime. Wires spilled from underneath most of the consoles, a result of various hacks and patches to keep the aging space ship running. Danica inhaled the scent of burning fuel that seemed to permeate the ship and felt a rush of affection for the bucket of bolts she'd practically grown up on.

"Looks like it," her pilot, Caro, said turning from one of the smaller consoles where she navigated the ship, her hair flying behind her as she spun back around. "And we're definitely outgunned."

"Can we out run them?" Danica asked as she made her way down to the center console and looked out at the massive ship blocking their escape.

"What we don't have in size or gun power, we make up for in maneuverability," Caro said. "Hold on."

"I hope you're right," Tori said from where she stood at the weapons console along the wall, her curly dark hair pulled up in a topknot and held in place with what looked like metal chopsticks with dangerously sharp ends—almost as sharp as her pointy teeth. Ridges formed a vee between her eyes—a hallmark of the Zevrians —making her look even fiercer than she was. "Because we're running low on weapons."

"How low?" Danica gripped the console with both hands as the ship jerked to the right and skirted underneath the larger ship.

"How good are you at hand-to-hand combat?" Tori asked, her brown muscled arms braced against the wall.

Danica had gotten a lot of flack—mostly from her father's old bounty hunter friends—when she'd brought on the Zevrian as her security chief, but she'd never had a moment's regret for making Tori a part of her team. Especially in situations like these.

"I thought we were supposed to stock up when we were docked at Centuri Twelve," Danica shouted over the roar of the engines firing.

"I would have if we had anything to buy them with," Tori said as the ship accelerated.

Danica sighed. Her crew had been running on fumes—sometimes literally—for weeks. "I know it's been tight, but once we turn over this bounty, we'll be flush for a while."

"I'm just glad Mourad won't have the satisfaction of beating us." Caro faced forward as the force of acceleration pressed her back into her chair. "I hate that guy."

Danica couldn't agree more. The ship shooting at them belonged to a bounty hunter and mercenary named Mourad who didn't believe in female bounty hunters and didn't believe in playing fair. Not that Danica was against stretching the rules or pushing her luck, but Mourad had no limits on what he and his crew would do to capture a bounty.

He was the one bounty hunter her father had gone out of his way to avoid because Mourad ignored all the usual professional courtesies and accepted practices. He would double-cross anyone. Instead of tracking down bounties himself, he was known for waiting until another bounty hunter did all the legwork, then he and his band of mercenaries would swoop in and snake the bounty. Just like he was trying to do now.

Over my dead body, Danica thought as their ship broke through the atmosphere and shot into space, the sky going from hazy yellow to inky blue to black. She thumped the side of the console, mentally thanking the ship for getting her out of yet another scrape.

When her father died, he'd left everything to her, which meant basically his ship. It had just been the three of them for as long as Danica could remember—her and her father and the ship. Crew had come and gone, but this ship had been the only constant in their lives aside from each other. She'd thought about selling it, but only for a moment. The old ship was as much a part of her as her father had been, and she couldn't stand the thought of losing both of them.

She knew her father had never wanted her to take over his bounty hunting business. Truth be told, he never thought it was possible, but after spending a childhood chasing after crooks all over the galaxy, she didn't really know any other life. She was good at tracking people and getting out of scrapes and skirting the law. Her father had taught her well.

Danica shook thoughts of her father out of her head as she glanced at the fuel gauge. "Good work. We should have enough steam to reach the Gendarvian outpost where we can unload out bounty and get our reward."

Tori crossed the bridge to stand next to her, the chain belt wrapped several times around her waist jingling as she walked. "I wonder what this one did to command such a high price."

Danica shrugged, tucking a loose strand of wavy blond hair behind her ear. "It's not our business to wonder why. I can tell you it wasn't for a violent offense. I've never had a bounty put up less of a fight."

"The tracking was the hard part. Dr. Max Dryden did a good job of hiding."

The women turned to see their engineer, Holly, step onto the bridge. While the rest of Danica's crew favored utilitarian clothes that made them look more like their male counterparts--military issue pants, T-shirts, multi-pocketed vests and jackets--the ship's engineer and computer whiz wore color and patterns and combined them fearlessly. Red hair spilled over her shoulders and down the skin-tight pink paisley top she'd paired over a equally snug pair of turquoise pants.

"Not good enough to outfox us," Tori said, hand on her hips.

"Luckily for you, I understand the doctor's research and narrowed it down to the few planets that are ideal for that type of scientific study," Holly said. "And then Bexli did her thing."

Bexli was the other non-human in the crew. A Lyciathian shape-shifter who excelled at sneaking in and out of otherwise impenetrable places, she was their ace in the hole. Officially, she was their acquisitions officer, but only in the sense that she could acquire any bounty by way of her shape-shifting skills. She was so indispensible, Danica even put up with the pet glurkin that Bexli had insisted on bringing on board.

"Remind me again what type of research," Tori said, then shook her head. "Never mind, I actually don't care."

Holly rolled her eyes at Tori. "The study of a rare mineral only found in a few systems. Word on the astro net is that the doctor has figured out a way to harness its power."

Caro twisted in her chair to face them. "I'm still not thrilled we're turning over a scientist. Are we sure this is a legit bounty? How many doctors do you know who commit crimes severe enough to command this amount?"

Danica frowned. She'd had the same thought and had been trying to ignore her inner voice during the entire search. "We don't have the luxury of picking and choosing our bounties. Anyway, if we don't turn the doctor in, someone else will. At least we treat our prisoners well."

"Not that all of them deserve it." Tori pulled up the hem of her black cargo pants to reveal a thin red scar running up her calf. "We should have put that Daxian smuggler out the airlock."

"Agreed," Bexli said as she joined the other women on the bridge, a tiny puff of green fur running along beside her. "He was particularly repulsive."

"Is the bounty all settled?" Danica asked.

Bexli nodded, and her iridescent lavender bob swung at her jawbone. "This one was a breeze. I didn't even have to transform into something terrifying to keep her in line."

She leaned against a console and scooped her pet glurkin, Pog, up in one arm, ruffling its fur and making it emit a low purr. "The Daxian only stopped struggling when I morphed into a gorvon."

"What's a gorvon?" Holly asked.

"A particularly gruesome creature from the Daxian's home world." Bexli grinned. "Lots of claws and fangs."

Caro laughed. "That explains why he soiled his cell."

"At least he kept us in fuel and rations for a month," Danica said, glancing at Tori. "And you gave him a few scars if I remember correctly."

Tori grinned. "A souvenir from the bounty hunter babes."

"You know I hate that nickname." Danica folded her arms across her chest.

"Babes is better than the other name they call us that also starts with a 'b.'" Holly leaned against one of the consoles, crossing her long legs at the ankles.

"I don't mind the name so much," Caro said. "At least they're talking about us."

Danica let out a long breath. "They should be talking about us because we've brought in the two highest bounties in the past astro-year, not because we're all women."

Holly patted her on the shoulder. "It's just because we're the first and so far only all-female bounty hunter crew. Once the novelty wears off or another crew comes along, people will talk about something else."

Danica knew there was truth in Holly's words, but she hated the fact that even though they'd brought in two of the toughest bounties around, the other hunters still didn't respect them. She'd known working in a field known for tough guys wouldn't be easy, but she'd hoped her unorthodox methods and maverick crew would win her respect. So far, they'd only managed to acquire nicknames.

"I say we own it," Tori said, taking one of the pointy chopsticks from her hair and pressing the needle-like point into the pad of her finger. "We know we can do any job the boys can do and, once we bring in this hot-shot doctor, we'll be rolling in enough dough to outfit this ship so we can blast anyone out of the sky. Let them call us babes then."

"Um, guys." Caro's fingers flew across the screen in front of her. "We probably shouldn't count our money quite yet."

Danica jerked her head to the screens above her, slamming her palm against the console when she saw the rival ship closing in on them. "I thought we had enough of a head start to lose them."

"They're faster than I expected for a ship that large," Caro said, maneuvering their ship so that it dipped to the left.

Holly slid onto the floor, landing with a thud. "A little warning next time."

"Sorry," Caro shouted over the sound of gunfire hitting their hull. "You should probably brace for impact."

A blast shook the ship and alarms began screaming, red lights flashing overhead.

"Was that a torpedo?" Danica asked, shaking her head in disbelief. Was a rival bounty hunter really trying to blow up her ship?

Holly scrambled to her feet, using the nearest console to pull herself toward the door. "I'd better get back to the engine. If we lose that, we're dead in the water."

"I'll go make sure the prisoner is okay," Bexli said, following Holly with Pog tucked under one arm.

The entire ship jolted and Danica heard the sound of metal scraping against metal. Her skin went cold. "They've clamped on."

Tori's face was grim. "They're boarding us."

"Maybe they'll take the doctor and go," Caro said, although her voice quivered.

Danica squeezed her hands into fists. "They're not taking our bounty." She turned to Tori. "Hold them off as long as you can, but don't get yourself killed. I have a plan."

Tori pulled the other chopstick from her hair and slipped both sharp metal sticks into her chain belt. "You got it, Captain."

Danica ran off the bridge and down the dimly lit corridor until she reached a steel door where Bexli stood guard. "I've got the doctor. Why don't you and Pog try to hold off Mourad's soldiers?"

Bexli nodded, her lithe frame and pale pink skin transforming into a hulking beast covered in matted fur with only the slightest hint of pink on the tips. Pog gave a gruff bark and became a green lizard the size of a human with short legs that scampered across the floor. Both creatures hurried off toward the noise of the enemy bounty hunters boarding their ship.

Danica turned back to the steel door and punched in a code. The door slid open with a groan, revealing a petite figure with short dark hair sitting on the edge of a cot in the sparse room.

"Doctor Dryden," Danica said, her breath ragged. "Some pretty nasty bounty hunters are coming on board to take you. I can promise you they won't be as humane as we've been, but I have a plan that could save us both."

The woman on the cot blinked her wide, blue eyes a few times before answering. "Call me Max."

CHAPTER TWO

Danica heard the booming footsteps reverberating off the floor as the crew from the rival ship came on board. "We only have a few minutes to make you look like one of us."

Max stood up. "What do you mean 'one of us'? Who are you?"

Danica managed a half smile. "I'm the captain of the galaxy's only all-female bounty hunting team."

"So you're the reason I'm being held against my will?" Max asked.

Danica gave a curt shake of her head. "You're focusing on the wrong thing, doctor. Unless you want to be dragged off this ship and thrown in a cell much less comfortable than this one, we need to convince the nastiest bounty hunter in the galaxy that you're part of my crew." Danica took off her own gray canvas vest and tossed it to the doctor. "Ditch that shirt and put this on."

Max eyed the zip-up vest with frayed edges. "Just this?"

Danica glanced at the brown pants the woman wore, glad they'd gotten dirty when she and Bexli had apprehended the doctor and brought her back to the ship. If she looked too neat and buttoned-up, the plan would never work.

"Would you ever wear just a vest?" Danica asked, searching her pants pockets and finding a black grease pencil she'd used as part of her camouflage on a recent mission.

"Not in a million astro-years."

"Perfect." Danica crossed to her. "The last thing we want you to look like is yourself."

The footsteps echoed off the metal corridors, causing Max's hands to shake as she pulled her white shirt over her head and slipped on the vest. Blaster fire was followed by roars and screams, and both women flinched.

"Were those your crew members?" Max asked.

Danica gave a quick shake of her head. "They're fine. They're just creating a distraction to give us more time." She grabbed the back of Max's head. "Hold still." She drew a thick black line under both of the doctor's blue eyes, extending each line out to make a cat eye. "There, that makes you look less uptight."

Max spit in her palms and ran her hands through her neatly parted hair, making it stand up. "How about that?"

Danica grinned. "Now you're starting to look like one of my crew." She squeezed the woman's arm. "Remember to look pissed off but not afraid. You're part of a badass female bounty hunter crew, you're not a scientist."

"To be honest, I am pissed off. Why did you drag me onto this ship, and why should I go along with your plan to pretend to be a part of your crew?"

Danica sighed. She did not have time for this. "I brought you on this ship because there's a massive bounty on your head. It's nothing personal."

Max's mouth fell open. "On my head? That's impossible. I'm a scientist."

"Yeah, I know." Danica put the grease pencil back in her pocket. "But the guys who've boarded my ship could care less. Trust me when I tell you that you do not want to be held captive by them."

Max studied her for a moment before nodding. "Okay, fine. And you are . . .?"

"Danica." Opening the door, Danica led the way into the corridor, pulling out her blaster and holding it in front of her with both hands.

"Do I need one of those?" Max asked, staying tucked behind her.

"Can you use one without blowing my head off?"

"Maybe not," Max admitted.

"Then let's hold off on that for a while." Danica put up a hand as the pounding footsteps came closer and caused the floor to tremble.

The two women held their position in the corridor as a group of three enormous creatures rounded the corner holding weapons almost as long as their arms. They were decked out in black pants and shirts that showed plenty of bicep, and their chests were draped with weapons and bullets. One had bumpy, purple skin, but she thought the other two were human.

"Drop it!" the man in front said when he saw Danica's blaster. He had a tattoo running up the back of his neck and a blond buzz cut.

Danica quickly assessed that she was outgunned and dropped her blaster to the floor. "Do you mind telling me why you boarded my ship? This is a violation of galactic--"

Her words were cut off as the man backhanded her, and she stumbled against the wall. Max screamed and backed up, then seemed to remember who she was supposed to be.

"Just who the hell do you think you are hitting my captain like that?" she yelled, helping Danica right herself.

"Looks like you need to learn when to keep your mouth shut too." The man lifted his arm to deliver a blow.

"Enough!" A deep voice made the man freeze and drop his arm. "They can't talk if you knock their teeth out."

Danica glared up at the owner of the deep voice, tasting the metallic tang of blood for the second time that day. "Mourad."

The tall, broad-shouldered man with a bald head, jaundiced skin, and completely black eyes grinned at her. He was a Gorglik, which meant that he had no body hair and spoke a language populated with sharp clicks, reminding her of an insect. The fact that he didn't blink confirmed the comparison. "You don't seem happy to see me."

Thanks to the universal translator implant she and all her crew had, she could understand him, although she wished she couldn't. "What do you want?" Danica spat out the words along with a mouthful of blood.

Mourad laid a thick hand on her shoulder. "Give me my rightful bounty, and we'll leave you and your sad little crew alone."

"Your bounty?" Danica tried to laugh, but her mouth ached. "How do you figure that?"

"It's taken us weeks to track you across the galaxy." Mourad shook his head. "And I'm not good at patience."

"So your plan is to follow us around and snake our bounties every time?" Danica asked.

Mourad shrugged. "If you can't manage to keep your prisoners, that's not my fault." The smile slipped off his face. "Now where is the doctor?"

"Do you see any doctor around here?" Danica swept her arms wide. "We didn't find him, Mourad. He wasn't on the planet."

The bounty hunter leaned close and his eyes became slits as he stared at Danica. "I don't believe you."

Danica turned her face slightly to avoid inhaling Mourad's foul breath. "You're welcome to search my ship, but you'll find no trace of a Dr. Max Dryden anywhere. If he was ever on that planet, he bugged out before we arrived."

"Then why did you try to outrun us?" Mourad asked.

"Gee." Danica tapped a finger against her chin. "Maybe because we didn't feel like being harassed by you and your goons."

Mourad straightened up, touching a comms link inside his ear.

"Anyone find the prisoner yet?" He frowned as he listened, then turned to his men. "Search every corner of this ship. If they're hiding my bounty, we'll find him, and then they'll all pay for our trouble."

The three men split up and ran off in two directions down the corridor as Mourad crossed his arms and stared at Danica and Max.

"You're wasting your time," Danica said. "From one bounty hunter to another, I'm telling you that we don't have him."

Mourad's lip curled into a sneer. "You're not a bounty hunter. You're a little girl pretending to be a bounty hunter."

Danica fought the urge to remind him of the two large bounties they'd brought in. It didn't do her any good to poke the bear. Or, in this case, the Gorglik.

"What about you?" Mourad turned his attention to Max. "You don't talk?"

"I'm fine with letting my captain do the talking," Max kept her voice steady.

"She's one of my engineers," Danica said. "She's still in training."

Mourad took in the petite woman. "A piece of advice? Find yourself another job." He let his eyes wander to the low neckline of her vest and stepped closer. "Better yet? A real warrior who can take care of you."

Max's cheeks flushed. Mourad took it as an encouraging sign and moved even closer until the pounding of footsteps interrupted him. He stepped away as his men came around the corner.

"Nothing, sir," Tattoo Neck said. "Our team searched everywhere. And it's not a large ship."

Mourad growled.

"I told you," Danica said. "The planet was a dead end."

Mourad's eyes rested on Danica. "I've left you alone for all this time out of respect for your father."

"You call this leaving me alone?" Danica spluttered. "Chasing us across the galaxy? Boarding our ship? Knocking me around? Trying to steal our bounty?"

Mourad leaned over her. "You and your crew have no business being bounty hunters."

Danica put a hand on her hip. "Well, that's not really your call, is it?"

Mourad spun on his heel. "Bring them."

Tattoo Neck took Danica by the arm and another thick-armed bounty hunter grabbed Max.

"You can't take us with you," Danica struggled as she was dragged along. "What are you going to do? Keep us in your brig the rest of our lives?" Her stomach dropped as she said it, and she hoped that wasn't his plan.

"No," Mourad said without turning around. "I'm going to maroon you and your crew on an uninhabited planet. It should slow you down long enough for me to nab this doctor and claim the half a million credits. Or you'll end up dying there." He craned his neck to meet Danica's eyes, giving her a smile that showed his yellow teeth. "Either way, you're out of my hair."

"Commander," Tattoo Neck said with a grin as evil as Mourad's. "We're close to the sand planet of Dandureen. Primitive society with no capability for space flight." His eyes flicked to Danica and Max, and he chuckled. "Last reported contact says their humanoid-compatible species is dwindling fast because they have few females."

Mourad threw his head back and laughed, the rough sound echoing off the steel walls. "Looks like you and your crew are about to be in high demand."

Danica swallowed hard and tried not to let her face betray her growing panic. It helped to focus her thoughts on one thing she knew for sure. One day she was going to kill Mourad.

CHAPTER THREE

Khalvek peered at the shifting sands in front of him. He'd spotted the faint movement from the top of the last dune he'd crested and now he sat perched above it, his long-bladed knife held tightly in one hand and his dark braid swinging over his shoulder and casting a pendulous shadow.

"You can't escape me," he murmured.

The golden sand moved again, leaving a swirling eddy, and Khalvek jabbed his knife down. He felt the blade make contact and thrust it deeper. The creature he'd impaled struggled for a minute, but Kahlvek used both hands to steady the knife as the writhing animal flailed under a layer of sand.

When all movement had stopped, he lifted the animal out of the ground with a twist of his hands. The light brown sand serpent was as long as his arm and almost as thick. He wrapped one hand around the struggling animal and it instantly stilled, lulled into a stupor by the energy pulses that made his people such skilled hunters. He silently thanked the creature for its sacrifice, pulled out his knife with his other hand, and took off the head with a single swipe of his blade. He admired the size of the creature before dropping it into the bag slung across his bare back and wiping his blade off on the leather straps wound around his muscled forearms. A drop of blood trickled onto his hand and he smeared it across the dark tribal tattoos covering one side of his chest.

Tilting his face up, he let the rays of the planet's two suns beat down on him, feeling satisfied. Now it looked like this was the hunting trip he'd claimed it to be. Not that he didn't enjoy hunting the elusive sand dwellers that hid during the day. He'd grown up tracking and searching for them, and was one of his tribe's best hunters. But hunting no longer fulfilled him the way revenge did.

He began moving toward the rock face that stretched across the sands and formed a natural and unspoken border between his people and their enemy. He hadn't seen any other creature for hours, aside from the sand serpent. Not many liked the solitude of the sands as he did, but it was the perfect place to quiet his mind and find escape. Escape he needed now more than ever.

He balled his hands into fists as he thought of why he'd left the oasis to trek by himself. Since his father's death almost a full solar rotation ago, he'd been unable to think of much else.

"You're obsessed," his cousin and best friend, Kush, had said when he'd told him of his plan.

"You think it is wrong for a son to avenge his father's death?" he'd snapped back at Kush. "I am a warrior like he was."

Kush had glared back at him, refusing to be intimidated by his taller and usually more aggressive kinsman. "And he was a great fighter who died a warrior's death in battle. Killing the Cresteks won't bring him back, and it will break the truce."

The truce. Khalvek couldn't think about it without his face darkening and his words turning to growls. His people were warriors, not keepers of peace. Especially not with creatures like the Cresteks. He hated that his father's successor had agreed to a truce. No matter what the new Dothvek leader promised, *he* would never forgive.

"If I cannot fight, I'd rather be on the sands hunting," he'd told Kush as he'd slid his knives into the leather strap across his chest and filled the water skins to prepare for his expedition.

Kush had looked at him with one dark, peaked eyebrow raised. "Hunting or spying on the Cresteks?"

Khalvek had shrugged, then placed a heavy hand on his cousin's shoulder. "I do nothing but watch and plan. For the moment."

"That is what worries me," Kush had said.

Even now, Khalvek felt his heart pound as he thought about taking his revenge on those who'd killed his father. He had no intention of wasting his life on vengeance that never came. He quickened his pace, anxious to reach the rocks before the suns set. He would have his revenge soon enough.

≈

To find out what happens when Danica's crew is marooned on Khalvek's planet, get BOUNTY today!

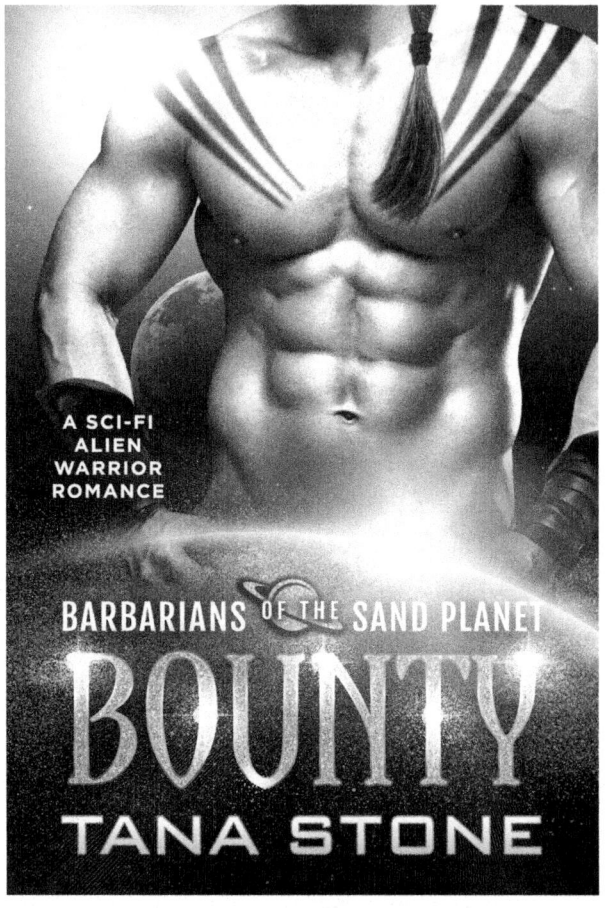

CLICK HERE TO GET IT NOW!

ALSO BY TANA STONE

The Tribute Brides of the Drexian Warriors Series:

TAMED (also available in AUDIO)

SEIZED (also available in AUDIO)

EXPOSED (also available in AUDIO)

RANSOMED (also available in AUDIO)

FORBIDDEN (also available in AUDIO)

BOUND (also available in AUDIO)

JINGLED (A Holiday Novella) (also in AUDIO)

CRAVED (also available in AUDIO)

STOLEN (also available in AUDIO)

SCARRED (also available in AUDIO)

ALIEN & MONSTER ONE-SHOTS:

ROGUE (also available in AUDIO)

VIXIN: STRANDED WITH AN ALIEN

SLIPPERY WHEN YETI

CHRISTMAS WITH AN ALIEN

YOOL

Raider Warlords of the Vandar Series:

POSSESSED (also available in AUDIO)

PLUNDERED (also available in AUDIO)

PILLAGED (also available in AUDIO)

PURSUED (also available in AUDIO)

PUNISHED (also available on AUDIO)

PROVOKED (also available in AUDIO)

PRODIGAL (also available in AUDIO)

PRISONER

PROTECTOR

PRINCE

The Barbarians of the Sand Planet Series:

BOUNTY (also available in AUDIO)

CAPTIVE (also available in AUDIO)

TORMENT (also available on AUDIO)

TRIBUTE (also available as AUDIO)

SAVAGE (also available in AUDIO)

CLAIM (also available on AUDIO)

CHERISH: A Holiday Baby Short (also available on AUDIO)

PRIZE (also available on AUDIO)

SECRET

RESCUE (appearing first in PETS IN SPACE #8)

Inferno Force of the Drexian Warriors:

IGNITE (also available on AUDIO)

SCORCH (also available on AUDIO)

BURN (also available on AUDIO)

BLAZE (also available on AUDIO)

FLAME (also available on AUDIO)

COMBUST

THE SKY CLAN OF THE TAORI:

SUBMIT (also available in AUDIO)

STALK (also available on AUDIO)

SEDUCE (also available on AUDIO)

SUBDUE

STORM

All the TANA STONE books available as audiobooks!

INFERNO FORCE OF THE DREXIAN WARRIORS:

IGNITE on AUDIBLE

SCORCH on AUDIBLE

BURN on AUDIBLE

BLAZE on AUDIBLE

FLAME on AUDIBLE

RAIDER WARLORDS OF THE VANDAR:

POSSESSED on AUDIBLE

PLUNDERED on AUDIBLE

PILLAGED on AUDIBLE

PURSUED on AUDIBLE

PUNISHED on AUDIBLE

PROVOKED on AUDIBLE

BARBARIANS OF THE SAND PLANET

BOUNTY on AUDIBLE

CAPTIVE on AUDIBLE

TORMENT on AUDIBLE

TRIBUTE on AUDIBLE

SAVAGE on AUDIBLE

CLAIM on AUDIBLE

CHERISH on AUDIBLE

TRIBUTE BRIDES OF THE DREXIAN WARRIORS

TAMED on AUDIBLE

SEIZED on AUDIBLE

EXPOSED on AUDIBLE

RANSOMED on AUDIBLE

FORBIDDEN on AUDIBLE

BOUND on AUDIBLE

JINGLED on AUDIBLE

CRAVED on AUDIBLE

STOLEN on AUDIBLE

SCARRED on AUDIBLE

SKY CLAN OF THE TAORI

SUBMIT on AUDIBLE

STALK on AUDIBLE

SEDUCE on AUDIBLE

ABOUT THE AUTHOR

Tana Stone is a USA Today bestselling sci-fi romance author who loves sexy aliens and independent heroines. Her favorite superhero is Thor (with Aquaman a close second because, well, Jason Momoa), her favorite dessert is key lime pie (okay, fine, *all* pie), and she loves Star Wars and Star Trek equally. She still laments the loss of *Firefly*.

She has one husband, two teenagers, and two neurotic cats. She sometimes wishes she could teleport to a holographic space station like the one in her tribute brides series (or maybe vacation at the oasis with the sand planet barbarians). :-)

She loves hearing from readers! Email her any questions or comments at tana@tanastone.com.

Want to join her VIP Readers list and be the first to know about contests and giveaways? Click here: BookHip.com/CRJHNH

Want to hang out with Tana in her private Facebook group? Join on all the fun at: https://www.facebook.com/groups/tanastonestributes/

facebook.com/tanastoneauthor

instagram.com/tanastoneauthor

bookbub.com/authors/tana-stone

amazon.com/Tana-Stone/e/B07V3LRSNH

Printed in Dunstable, United Kingdom